HONOR AMONGST THIEVES

BOOK ONE: ABANDONED NATION

WRITTEN BY

A. C. CLAYTON

HONOR AMONGST THIEVES

Copyright © Sharieff Clayton, 2007.
All rights reserved.

Published by

Amenta Publications, LLC

International Standard Book Number (ISBN)
paper: 0-9796731-0-8

Printed in the United States of America

Without limiting the rights under copyright reserved above, no part of this publication may be reproduced, stored in or introduced into a retrieval system, or transmitted, in any form, or by any means (electronic, mechanical, photocopying, recording or otherwise), without the prior written permission of both the copyright owner and the above publisher of this book.

This book is dedicated my family for all you unwavering support during dark times: Love and Loyalty is all we breed. Without you Amenta would never be.

To Hoduri (Razor) Sutherland and Jermaine (O.P.) Akwa. Man I'm still at a lost for words. I miss you guys. To all the fallen warriors whose stumbles, miscalculations and untimely departures made this equation inevitable. To all the prisoners locked behind bars; there must come a time when free lunch must be despised!

To All my Kings and Queens (my Comrades) whose lives I touched and who have had and impact on my life; we know the truth there is

HONOR AMONGST THIEVES

Stand firm!
Behind every great fortune, lurks an even greater crime.
Sad but it's the <u>American</u> way.

Honor Amongst Thieves

Foreword

First, I am honestly honored to have been able to walk with, talk with, and ultimately become comrades with Mr. A. C. Clayton, the author of this book. When he handed me a copy of Honor Amongst Thieves I really didn't know what to expect being that we had very little correspondence since walking the yard in a maximum-security prison almost a decade ago. I was also skeptical because there are so many corny hood novels in this market right now that I truly grew disinterested in reading any of them. But I knew that if anyone could capture the hood, it would be A.C. Clayton. Highly intelligent, I've personally witnessed him turn a group of young wild adolescents (while still an adolescent himself), into a group of avid readers with the desire to learn and eventually become strong minded young men. But still I never thought he would actually write such a powerful book. I can definitely say I didn't expect to read such a vivid depiction of the life of a young man torn between being a product of his environment and becoming in tune with his own conscience.

The young man I speak about is the main character of this book, Kameek "Kay-Kay" Barnes. A young man who grew up in the rough streets of Brooklyn, New York and involved himself in every aspect of a lifestyle we call, The Game. From robbery to selling drugs to murder, Kay-Kay follows the footsteps of his older Brother Jamal, as they both experience the ins and outs as well as the ups and downs of committing themselves to the code of the streets. It wouldn't be long before Kay-Kay would find himself incarcerated, learning the difference between walking the wild and crazy halls of Rikers Island's infamous C-74 to dodging multiple attempts on his life in a number of maximum-security prisons.
Unfortunately, for so many young Black and Latino men, the sad reality is that incarceration has become the place where boys become men. Kay-Kay reflects this reality, as

those who would school him do, with hopes that he would somehow change the game. On his journey, he meets a hood icon known as the "Old God". A legend who had been in prison before Kay-Kay was born. This would be the most life-altering encounter of his young life. Under the Old God's tutelage Kay-Kay learns the difference between being a boy and becoming a man. As you read this book, you will get as close to a first hand experience, as possible, to what a lot of rappers, actors and others try to depict in their music and movies.

This is a story told by someone who has experienced all of what you will read first-hand. He has been Kay-Kay, he has been the Old God, and he has also been Jamal. Get ready for a reading experience of a lifetime - trust and believe you can't get this from a gangster rap song or a menace to society type movie. THIS IS AN OFFICIAL ISSUE. I proudly introduce one of the most powerful books I've read in my life. Written by one of the most powerful men I've ever met in my life...Honor Amongst Thieves... Book One - Abandoned Nation.

Brian "Saigon" Carenard

Honor Amongst Thieves

Remember when I taught you how to roll dice?

Remember when I took you on that first heist?

I taught you to always keep the jewels that was flooded with ice

Most important of all, I taught you to never sleep in Ghetto's paradise

Who would've thought then that you would become what you are

That center of gravity That star amongst stars

Stay focused youngblood on all that got you there

The selfless sacrifices and the countless tears

I write you these words because you now sit on the throne

Stay vigilant youngblood 'cause even the best can be overthrown

PROLOGUE

    Five days of deliberation and the so-called jury of my peers have still failed to reach a verdict. I guess, at the very least, I should feel apprehensive and worried when in truth I feel none of that. For the past fourteen months, I've been held incommunicado with only my wife, children and attorney who were allowed to visit. I've been confined in a state of the art tin cell, equipped with a built in shower and a caged recreation area attached to its back door. In this cage, I am allowed one hour daily to roam freely. I have been denied phone privileges under the pretense that I *still wield considerable power within an elusive crime syndicate that seems to have more heads than a hydra.*
    Despite all the hype and their spirit breaking tactics, I am truly at peace and I believe that my indifference is what truly bothers the prosecution. The media coverage has been sensational. After fourteen months, I am still headline news. *"There's no escape!"* read The N.Y. Post the day my trial began. *"Guilty Verdict a Gavel Beat Away!"* predicted the Daily News when deliberations began. One reporter – Peter some – shit from the N.Y. Times wrote, "...it's not a question of whether or not Kameek "Kay-Kay" Barnes (that's me) is guilty. The question is whether the prosecution successfully proves his guilt beyond a reasonable doubt." After reading that line I understood O.J's plight better. The truth is no one, not even the judge, knows which way this jury will swing.

Honor Amongst Thieves

Since the day of my arrest there have been all sorts of stories and mini-biographies about my life; unnamed eyewitness accounts of my 'rise to the top'. My lawyer has received countless requests for interviews, as well as four different movie offers. I have rejected them all. My decision to do so has little to do with my lawyer's sound advice; the truth is far more complex than that. I am from a dying, perhaps distinct breed; a breed that holds water no matter the holes. I have nothing to say to the media or their mind controlled readers. My life story ain't made for closed-caption. What makes my saga so appealing is the million-dollar question – how? A question they will never know the answer to. How was I able to do it undetected? How could the streets, a virtual chatterbox, fall silent at the mere mention of my name? Am I a villain or a hero? Am I a sinner or a saint?

Only you, my imaginary companion who's toiled with me in this 12 x 16 tomb for the past fourteen months, will hear the how and the why of it all. Hero or villain? Perhaps both – it is for you to decide. With one jury knee deep in deliberation, another, more wiser, will now hear all the facts.

PART ONE

CHAPTER 1
THE ROAD TO NOWHERE

Three eardrum-shattering gunshots echo in my mind as I relive the day it all began. My very first robbery...I was twelve. Twenty-two years ago, I embarked on a journey that has led me to both heaven and now hell. Exposure to such a ruthless way of life at a young age has led me to this solitary confinement I now find myself in.

July 1982...a scorcher. The stifling and suffocating heat of the day still plays vivid and crystal clear in my mind. It was only 80 something but in New York City, the humidity made 80 something feel like 105 degrees easily. Personally, I've always loved the heat and the sun kissing my flesh. I just hated the humidity. I was hanging out with my brother Jamal, nicknamed *J.B*, three years my senior. An artist consumed with a passion to write and draw graffiti. Man...he was something else when it came to bombing.

Already a recognized figure in the underworld of graffiti writers, he was a mystery to so many artists, most of whom were his elders by years. For him, *3-D* was for toys and wild-style was the way he did his homework. J.B. drew entire *sagas*.

Those in the graffiti world, especially those from back in the day, know what is being spoken of here. It is only those individuals who appreciated my brother's contribution. My brother also went around crossing out or boofing other writers' tags if he considered them toys. He would then write his tag to let them know who dissed them - this is why it was imperative for him to remain a mystery to most.

I loved hanging out with him when he went bombing because an adventure was always guaranteed. We were forever being chased by police and super heroes; those who would go out of their way to try to stop us from escaping. J.B.'s closest friend Robert was also known as *Knee*. Knee hated for anyone to refer to him as a pretty boy - to him that was the ultimate insult - only sissies tried to be pretty. Those who knew him would never refer to him as being a pretty boy, but he was and it was obvious. His peanut butter complexion afforded him the title *golden boy* amongst the girls. His delicate hawk-like features always made him a female's first choice. Seventeen years old and already his acclaim as a stick up kid was infamous. If there was ever a true stick up kid that existed, he was the shining star...a role model for it. His older brothers were upstate in prison serving life sentences for charges I didn't know existed at the time. Needless to say, this gave Knee undivided props with the older kats in the hood. Everywhere Knee went he kept a *Roscoe* on him. (Oh! My bad...back then we called guns Roscoes.) He inherited a closet full of Roscoes when his brothers passed on to their living graves. This particular day, Knee had a 38 Special with only three bullets in its barrel.

"*I got the shit all staked out! The Dred leaves his weed under a garbage can and keeps his loot in his socks.*"
Knee was hyped as he laid out his plan. J.B. didn't want to go and was trying to come up with an excuse.

"*What about my little brother? He's only twelve.*"
"*Man...Kay-Kay can come with us.*"
Before J.B. could respond, I spoke up.
"*I'm with it. Let's go!*"

J.B. gave me that *I'm gonna fuck you up when we get home* look but I paid it no mind. Besides, home was a long way off at the moment. 8:30 p.m., the sun was beginning to set as we marched up Church Avenue until we hit the corner of East 21st Street. There he was...the Dred; in his early twenties, six feet tall, stocky with thick long locs, which hung like vines past his waist, smoking a spliff.

Though the sun could not be seen anymore, he wore dark shades. As we neared him, I could smell the pungent aroma of the ganja lingering in the atmosphere. It blended nauseously with the smell of urine and vomit coming from somewhere nearby. The block sported two corner stores and a bunch of four story apartment buildings. Trash was scattered everywhere, a typical block in this area of Flatbush. As we approached, my heart began to pump furiously. Rapper's Delight blared from a second floor window. Too late to run, I had to stay calm and look cool just like Knee said. The plan was laid down and nothing could go wrong...or could it? Knee didn't hesitate. He pulled the 38 Special out, aimed it at the Dred, cocked it and yelled...

"*You know what the fuck this is!*"

The Dred stayed still, his face revealing no emotion. *Oh shit! This is really happening!* I ran and lifted up the garbage can looking for the weed. I heard Knee tell the Dred to turn the fuck around and put his hands on the wall. The Dred must have hesitated because Knee repeated himself with a warning included. I felt it. Something just wasn't right. Meanwhile J.B. began to search the Dred from head to toe. As he reached the Dred's socks, he felt the bulge. J.B. stuck his hand inside the Dred's socks and pulled out a wad of rolled up bills. Excitedly he yelled...

"*I got it! Let's go!*"

I, on the other hand, still couldn't find the weed. All I saw were paper bags scattered everywhere.

"*Did you find it yet?*" Knee asked.

"*Nah man. Ain't nothing here but paper bags.* The tension was thick in the air. My heart felt like it was ready to explode.

"*Check the bags!*" Knee growled, every word dripping with impatience. A few seconds later...

"*I got it!*"

The paper bag containing the weed was lying all that time next to my left foot. The bag was filled with many small plastic baggies, each bag containing a portion of weed. We began to relax preparing to make our exit when the Dred decided to turn around. In our excitement, none of us noticed his movement. The Dred sprang off the wall cursing...

"*Blood clot!*"

Knee's reflexes were remarkable. He stepped back and fired in one fluid motion - BLAM! **BLAM! BLAM!** Click, Click, Click - no more bullets. The Dred was down on his knees holding his stomach, his head, as if in prayer, bowed to the ground. Deathly afraid, I took off and was so scared that I dropped the bag with the weed in it, without even realizing. J.B. and Knee also took flight. As I ran, I noticed people coming out of the stores to see what had happened. I heard their screams, but who would look back? Not me amigo, I kept running. I felt as though I was running on air. I was running fast and hard. Sirens gave off a distinct and ominous cry. My breath was lost. I rolled underneath a parked car and hid. I had to rest.

*   *   *

CHAPTER 2
TAKING PAPERS

So many years ago, yet the memory of that day is still so vivid. It's funny how we are able to remember so many distant episodes in our lives, but fail to recall the most trivial event that happened just yesterday. Nonetheless, I would say from that point on, my life was about taking papers. The following two years went by like a blur. Everyday we went on a mission looking for *vics;* picking herbs we called it. We were pretty successful in most of our endeavors until we picked the right herb at the wrong time. He was a Pee Wee Herman looking muthafucka walking away from the bank's ATM machine. The caper appeared simple. Little did we know, Pee Wee Herman was under surveillance by the Feds. For what? To this day I haven't a clue.

We converged on the insect like a lotus, boxing our prey up against the bank's wall. He was visibly afraid. Knee pointed the Chrome .32 automatic at Pee Wee and demanded money. Pee Wee immediately complied. Like I said it was a piece of cake - in and out. Yet before we knew what hit us, undercover pigs were everywhere yelling...

"*Drop the fucking weapon! Now!* "

Man...they didn't have to tell my boy Knee twice. He dropped the gun like it was hot and put his hands in the air. J.B. was only a split second behind Knee putting his hands in the air also. You would think I would simply follow suit. Instead I faked a jack as if I were about to surrender and took flight...or tried to at least. Before I could get ten full steps in, a blow to the side of my head put me down for the count. I felt sharp kicks to my back and stomach. I kicked back. Ah man...why did I do that shit? A foot to my mouth dazed me. J.B. and Knee tried to come to my aide. Before I knew it all three of us were lying on the ground in fetal positions trying to protect ourselves from deadly kicks and stomps.

"*You stupid fucking niggers! You monkey bastards!*"

Were some of the rights read to us. The only thing that stopped these would-be lynchers from conforming too far back to their true nature was that the entire ordeal drew the attention of many bystanders who were yelling for the pigs to stop. They stopped their assault on us, handcuffed us and left us on the cold ground for what felt like hours.

Eventually the NYPD arrived, took us into custody and on to the hospital for treatment of the minor bruises we acquired, as a result of the courtesy, professionalism and respect bestowed upon us by the Feds. We were charged with armed robbery in the first degree, assault of a peace officer, grand larceny and interfering with a federal investigation - which was dropped before the case ever went

to the grand jury. Because I was fourteen at the time, a minor, I was put in the precinct's bullpen.

With a tight grip on my earlobe I was escorted out of the precinct by my moms. Boy was she mad! A flood of obscenities escaped her lips.

"Thieves...fuckin' thieves. I bust my ass for eight hours everyday just to raise thieves."

"But Ma...we're innocent."

Whack! From out of nowhere her free hand found my forehead. I tried to dodge it at the last second but her other hand was still super glued to my ear.

"Now you wanna start lying. First a thief - now a liar."

The rising crescendo of her voice was my only warning. Whack! I was able to block the second blow, though the first one found its target. My bottom lip became numb and I could already taste the blood on my tongue. Definitely time for a new tactic.

"I'm sorry Ma, we didn't mean it."

"You didn't mean it?"

She swung again, a little slower this time. I was able to block the blow with ease. *Perhaps she was getting tired.* Deciding not to tempt fate I wisely shut up. The entire way home my moms held on to my ear like a trophy. People looked on, giving her sympathetic nods, as if she were the one whose ear had grown numb. It sounds crazy, but at that moment I envied my brother.

J.B. and Knee were on their way to central booking. In two days they would be inmates on their way to Rikers Island, C-74 to be exact. *Just to hear the name makes your spine tingle. This is a jungle where the murderers mingle.* A few dudes from my hood had been there and came home with razor scars we called *blasts* on their faces and *bozo boots* two - three sizes too big for them. These were the boots given to them after being robbed for their original footwear. I was minutely worried about J.B. and Knee. They were cut from a different cloth. Both had heart and learned a bit of the 52 fighting style from Knee's older brother *Swift*. They were two of the best fighters for their age in my hood.

The first visit to Rikers Island my moms went alone. She was adamant about not letting me go. That was until the indictments began to fall. Four more people picked us out of a mug shot book for robberies and before we knew it, we were fighting five cases.

Knee wanted to take every case to trial, while J.B. wanted to cop out. As for me, I was pretty indifferent. The fact that I was out, still roaming…still stalking…still taking papers…made the cases seem unreal. On my first visit to Rikers, I learned that on their very first night there, J.B. and Knee had a small skirmish with the other prisoners. However, after that day, it was smooth sailing for them.

Knee was well known, primarily because of his older brothers and because his reputation preceded him.

Kats who didn't know Knee by face, knew him by name. However, Knee didn't stay in general population long. His second week on the Island ended with him cutting a dude in the face over the phone and straight to the bing he went. J.B., on the other hand, was seriously studying law. Everyday he was in the Law Library looking for loopholes in the cases against us. Every visit he would tell my Mother and me what he discovered and every time he seemed more convinced that a plea bargain was our only solution.

HONOR amongst THIEVES

The problem was Knee. Copping out was a *no-no* in his *book of thugging*. According to Knee, none of his brothers ever copped out. Of course, this was not true. I discovered years later that his oldest brother *Gunz* gave information on a homicide that took place in Attica. But that's another story. J.B. and Knee were facing 25 to life for all the charges. Knee's only response to this news was...
"Fuck it - all the way baby! All the way!"
He was determined to go to trial. J.B. and Knee fought each other on their way to court one day behind this. The situation was if J.B. and I copped out, we would have to implicate Knee. This was not an option so we had to figure out a way to convince Knee to cop out. I spoke with him, my moms spoke with him; both attempts proved futile. My moms left the visit convinced that Knee was a psychopath. From that day on, she referred to him as being *stark raving mad* and warned J.B. that Knee would be the death of him. We had no clue how to convince Knee that he had to take a plea. I stumbled onto the solution rather painfully.

Four months passed since our arrests. Knee was back in the box while J.B. received his GED. Despite the circumstances, my moms was extremely proud of him. Their relationship had grown pretty tight since J.B.'s incarceration. As for me, while accompanying my mother on the visits my job was to bring J.B. and Knee weed, razors (*gem stars*) as well as convince chicks from around the way to visit them. One chick named *Gwen* turned up pregnant by Knee and he was bragging about becoming a father. J.B. calmly explained to Knee that his baby would be at least twenty-five when and if they made it home. Knee still wouldn't listen. As for me...I was still taking papers. In fact, I was beginning to realize that the solo act was more lucrative and safe. I was more of a schemer...a strategist. If I didn't see an escape route I wouldn't tempt fate, at least not up until that point I didn't.

*   *   *

CHAPTER 3
DILEMMAS AND SOLUTIONS

1985 exploded on the scene with crack houses everywhere. Drug dealers began flaunting their newfound success with new cars and big jewelry. This was all good because I was determined to capitalize off of their success as well.

I had been messing with this doe-eyed dime piece named *Precious* on the other side of town. She lived in the projects, which is why anytime I went to see her, Roscoe became my companion. One night while leaving her crib, I found myself walking mad blocks trying to flag down a cab. It was late, around 1 a.m. and in that part of the hood, cabs seldom stopped for young black teens. Only the most daring or desperate cabbies did. To this day I haven't figured out which. As I passed one block, I noticed something that forced me to double back. What I saw immediately made my palms sweaty. In the middle of this darkly lit block stood a man with either 100 gold chains around his neck or something even better - a dookie rope. At this time only a handful of drug dealers had these and an even smaller percent of rappers. Yet, to wear something like that at that time of night in Brooklyn was lunacy.

Whatever the case, this joker was about to be had; I quickly crossed the street. Now on the opposite side of the street from him, my anticipation began rising like an erection. I paused and put a slug in the chamber of my .25 automatic Raven. Prepared to kill for the chain, I ducked low and began jogging toward my prey. Three cars away…two…one car away…I paused again. The prey was directly across the street from me. He was at that moment facing my direction, but could not see me hiding behind the car.

A chick was sitting on the car in front of him. *So that's why he's out here so vulnerable, trying to impress sis.* I was able (while I waited for him patiently to turn back toward sis) to see the chain up close. The shit was huge! Instead of one dookie rope, it was two ropes supporting one medallion. The medallion was of some kind of bird but I wasn't sure. I was still too far off to see details. *Damn! Would my pounding heart give my location away?* No sooner had the thought crossed my mind to abort the mission out of fear, did the joker turned back toward the chick, giving me the drop I was waiting for. Emerging from behind the car with my gun already aimed toward his head, the chick saw me coming. Just as I anticipated, she was completely stuck in a prison of disbelief and fear. Joker must have read her face because he turned swiftly.

He began to reach for his waist but changed his mind quickly. He must have seen the determination, lust and death in my eyes, for it was surely there. Never before had I been this serious about scoring. For me this was a do or die move. I believe he read this energy and understood his position. Resistance was futile. He put his hands up and said...

"You got it shorty. Just don't hurt me."

I ordered the chick to take his gun slowly out of his waist. The bitch was too slow and I told her so. She moved at a speed more to my satisfaction when I told her to place the gun behind her on the roof of the car...she complied. *Good girl.* Then I told her to take the chain from around joker's neck and put it right next to the gun. I asked joker if he had any money. He shook his head affirmatively. I told her to dig in his pockets and pull everything out: a lighter, wallet, a set of keys and a knot of money. I ordered her to put the money on the roof of the car next to the gun and chain. As I advanced I instructed them both to back away slowly. Joker finally mustered enough courage to speak.

"*Yo shorty. Just tell me who sent you. Was it that nigga Pop? Word to mutha shorty, you can keep everything. I just wanna know who snaked me.*"

By this time his gun was securely on my waist, his chain dangling from my neck and his money was about to vanish into my pocket when he asked...

"*Yo shorty. You know who the fuck I am? Anywhere you go shorty I'll...*"

BLAM!! He never finished. I fired. The bitch screamed. He ran and so did I - in the opposite direction. I didn't shoot to kill him; I already had what I came for. I just wanted to shut him up before he got bold enough to make me shoot him. I ran to the opposite corner from which I came. In my thirst to rob this clown, I hadn't formulated an escape route or plan and found myself running back toward Precious' crib. As I was running, I decided Precious' crib was the best course of action. I knew she was still awake. Her moms was out chasing that crack and Precious nor her little brother or sister would go to sleep until their moms returned safely.

Precious opened the door surprised to see me. I walked in still very winded, with the chain dangling around my neck.

"*God damn! What you do, rob a rapper?*"

"*Nah. Just a joker.*"

She ran to the phone that was lying on the couch.

"*Girl, I'll call you back later. That was Kay-Kay at the door...I don't know...I'll call you back.*"

She hung up. Before she could ask a million and one questions, I pulled the mint out. There were a bunch of tens at the top. As I kept peeling, the bills grew larger. *Damn...this joker was loaded.* I slipped off a $50 and handed it to Precious. I told her to go get some Chinese and junk food for us and the kids.

I got on the phone and called my crib. My moms picked up. I told her I was safe but stranded at Precious' house because of the cab situation. She began reading me the riot act about being irresponsible. I was half listening because I was counting the mint. Minus the 50 bucks I gave Precious, I had a little less than $4800. I took the chain from around my neck and began examining it. The shit was heavy. The medallion - a ruby-eyed eagle clutching a diamond chipped sword. *Damn...this was by far the biggest caper I ever pulled off.*

Just then my moms said she would see me in the morning. I agreed, hung up, laid my head on the pillow and waited for Precious to return, wishing J.B. and Knee were here. We would've undoubtedly taken turns rockin' the chain. I had to take pictures of it for them. Matter of fact, I decided I'd wear it up on the visit and let them take flicks with it on. *Damn I came off!* I was laying there with two guns on my waist, damn near five g's in my pocket, and a big chain around my neck waiting

for some Chinese food and some pussy thinking to myself - *Who was that joker?* Little did I know I wouldn't wonder for long.
    *   *   *

CHAPTER 4
JOKERS ARE WILD

Downtown's Albee Square Mall's game room was a thief's den. Crooks from all areas of Brooklyn met, mingled and at times settled beefs there. It was like a disorganized thieves' guild.

With my latest and flashiest acquisition around my neck, I stepped into the den nonchalantly. Usually I headed straight to Ms. Pac-Man in the back of the game room but I knew better than to leave my back exposed to these cutthroats for too long. My purpose, like any other crook of my small caliber at that time, was to simply show off. And show off I did. All heads turned immediately appraising, acknowledging and scheming. Most of these kats I knew by face. Like me…none were of high rank. They were clawing their way up the ladder, yet unlike me, they didn't use guns. I discovered this flaw the previous year on Easter when Knee and I went out to Coney Island…

*   *   *

Coney Island's official opening was always on Easter. On this day, thousands traveled to and congregated there. The daytime was for parents and their kids. The night belonged to the Knights. Knee and I went out there looking for vics. Instead I met Precious.

Nevertheless, the gangsters were out. Posses from every hood were representing. Even the big dogs walked cautiously on this day because they understood, in the most primitive sense, how easily predators could become prey. The word was spreading that there were too many police out. One posse was heading for the Deuce (Times Square). Knee and I decided to go with them. Midtown always proved a lucrative endeavor.

H♀N♀R amongst THiEVES

> As soon as the train pulled in and the doors opened onto the Midtown station we went up the stairs and down 7th Avenue. It was sheer pandemonium. Wolf pack was an excellent terminology given to this. We were around eighty deep. Anything in our path felt the wrath. It was like a grab bag until one vic pulled out a gun refusing to get robbed. Knee immediately drew his Roscoe in response. The rest of the crimeys began yelling GUN! And suddenly seventy-eight muthafuckas were off to the races leaving me, Knee and the rebellious vic staring at each other. The police were coming so the Mexican standoff ended peacefully. Knee and I stayed close and made it home with no real difficulty. A lot of dudes weren't as lucky. They got rounded up that night...

*   *   *

These were some of the seventy-eight faces I saw as I passed through the game room. Before they could formulate a plan, I broke out. I walked through the mall like a celebrity. I even went so far in my theatrics as to wave to strangers at a distance as if I knew them. I was stunting and enjoying every minute of it. After leaving the mall I walked up Fulton Street until I reached a sneaker store called *Dr. Jay's*. One look at my chain spelled money to the manager. The world revolves around predator and prey. Dr. Jay's was no different. I went in the store to buy J.B. and Knee a pair of sneakers and was in no mood to be conned into shopping. I told the manager so and he respectfully backed off. After buying two pairs of Jordans I exited the store and immediately spotted a glitch in the Matrix. One of those lustful faces I left behind in the game room was standing not too far off acting like he was waiting on a bus. *Amateurs!* I turned right and began stepping. I didn't need to look back to know I was being followed.

When I reached the corner I took another right and began walking down a small quiet block. I can imagine how excited this must have made those kats feel when unexpectedly I dipped into another store, a bookstore. I was having fun like a cat does when toying with a mouse. It has it cornered and begins to play with it before devouring it. How quickly the tables were going to turn on these characters in a matter of minutes. J.B. was growing into an avid reader and he wanted me to pick up a few books for him. I can't recall all three of the books I bought that day but I know one was <u>Destruction of the Black Civilization</u>. The hospitality in that particular bookstore was always homely and so I left with warm words of departure from the owners.

Walking out of the store, I noticed how desperate these characters had become. Where there was once one overt spotter, there were now three trying to act nonchalant. They must have figured I would turn left, head back toward Fulton Street and the safety of the crowd. They were apparently prepared to prevent that. All three were positioned to stop me from reaching Fulton. Instead I turned right and picked up my pace. I couldn't help but look back and was amazed how three guys quickly materialized into fifteen. This game we played reminded me of red light, green light, one…two…three…and I decided to play along for one more block.

Crossing Jay Street I continued straight, taking me deeper into a remote area of very little human activities. No sooner had I made it to the middle of the block did they decide to strike.

"*A yo…Kay-Kay!*"…one of the characters called as they began speeding up. I lowered my bags to the ground and spun around to face them. They stopped in their tracks, like I said…red light, green light!

"*What's up!*"?

In the same moment I pulled out my .25 automatic. Their eyes lit up. Like I said, they weren't big dogs.

"*So ya'll muthafuckas wanna rob me, huh?*"

"*Nah…nah man!*"

BOOM!! I fired. **BOOM!! BOOM!! BOOM!! BOOM!!** I let off five or six rounds directly at them. I saw one go down. The others were high tailing it up out of dodge. I picked up my bags and ran straight to Nevins Street. When I reached Nevins, I made way toward the Jay Street/Borough Hall train station when I heard sirens. It sounded like they were close. At the last minute I decided not to go into the train station feeling that it

HONOR amongst THIEVES

might be a trap off. Next to Jay Street there is a park of some sort with bushes and benches. With not a moment to spare I threw the Roscoe in the bushes just before the police cars flew by. I then tucked the chain in the bag with the sneakers and began to walk toward the court building; the opposite direction from where the shots were fired.

As I walked by the Supreme Court, I decided it would be an excellent hide out. I entered the building walked through the metal detectors, up the elevator and into the first courtroom I saw. There I chilled for three hours observing justice at its finest, oblivious to the manhunt that was taking place. It wasn't until I made it home and saw the story on the news that I found out the police were looking for a man with a gun, wearing a big chain who shot a would be thief in the stomach. I wasn't worried. Those kats wouldn't talk to the police. However, in the streets, nothing goes unnoticed and so I knew the beef was on.
Throughout the day my beeper kept going off with a 411 signal followed by Precious' number. I knew what she wanted. I promised her the night before that I would take her shopping that day. She also said she had something important to talk to me about, but I knew it would be nothing but a sob story, a way for her to get more money than I was willing to give. I liked Precious a lot, perhaps loved her, but I loved money more and I wasn't ready to part with it so easily. I decided not to respond to her beeps.

There was a wannabe gunrunner on my block named *Dave*. Once, Knee gassed J.B. into buying a .32 automatic from him. Dave swore up and down the .32 was brand new. We found out soon enough that it wasn't. Anyway Dave claimed he had a bulletproof vest for sale. I went to check him and we found ourselves on the roof of his building where he made all of his transactions. He wanted $500 for the vest. I wanted the vest tested. He wanted to lay it on the roof's floor and shoot it. I wanted him to strap it on and let me shoot him. He found it funny and so did I at first, but the more I thought about it and that fucked up gun he sold my brother, the more serious I became.

"Stop playin'!"

"I ain't playin'. If it's as good as you say it is, then you won't feel a thing...right or wrong?"
"Yeah, but you never know."
We were at an impasse. I really wanted the vest and his hesitancy at trying it on gave me an advantage.
"Ayat. I'll tell you what. I'll take your word for it that it works, but I'm only giving you $300."
"$350..."
I agreed. The following afternoon, I found myself on the visiting room floor at Rikers Island with a fake ID I secured from the Deuce. The ID placed my age at nineteen. Back in those days you could visit two prisoners at the same time. I was now able to visit my brother and Knee without a guardian. Heads began to turn as I walked into the visiting room with my new acquisition. Prisoners looked on with a tempting curiosity. Their visitors, mostly women, looked at me with a little something more than a casual glance. I figured I was receiving all of this attention because I looked older than my fifteen years. I took a seat and waited. J.B. and Knee entered the visiting room about twenty minutes later.

When they saw me, their faces lit up. Not only were they surprised to see me without moms, it was also the size of the chain I had dangling from my neck that caught their eye. A chain they knew I obtained the Brooklyn way. In the hood, most thieves need teams to score. When one can score big on his own without the back up of others, he is considered exceptional. Knee began to laugh. A laughter that was always infectious.

"Yo...how'd you get up here without Ma", J.B. asked but before I could answer Knee jumped in...
"Man fuck that! What up with this?"
He was cradling the medallion in his hands, appraising the craftsmanship. Knee's admiration brought a smile to my face. I could see it in his eyes - pride and envy. He lifted the double chain over my head and off my neck, weighing the trophy trying to estimate its worth.
"Damn this is at least a buck eighty", Knee took and educated guess.
"Close" I grinned.

"*How close?*"

"*213...*"

We were talking pennyweights - the weight used to measure gold. At $11 a pennyweight we were looking at a base value of $2300. If I chose to sell the chain back to a jewelry store I could easily get $3000 for it. J.B. took the chain from Knee as if he didn't believe it was really that heavy.

"*Damn. I thought these shits were supposed to be hollow?*"

"*Yeah...I thought so too.*"

"*Man who's the clown who got caught slippin' with dis?*"

Knee wanted details.

"*Not a clown...a joker.*" I responded.

"*Same shit.*"

Knee dismissed my word semantics with a contemptuous wave of his hands. In detail, I began explaining the heist. Knee kept shaking his head wishing he had been there. J.B. also shook his head; a little slower though, as if gravity itself was his archenemy. I knew my brother well enough to know that what appeared to be a battle with the natural law of physics was in truth a struggle with his own conscience. Like Dr. Frankenstein regretting his creation, J.B. always regretted taking me with him that hot summer day.

"*Yo...I left some dough in ya account and got ya those pair of Jordans we spoke about.*"

"*Good lookin'.*"

Knee shot a friendly jab to my chin. J.B. shook his head in gratitude yet remained silent.

"*So who's this chick Precious? Is that the chick with the fat ass you met at Coney Island?*"

"*Yeah.*"

"*Yo J.B. Your little brother got some good taste.*"

"*You serious about her?*" J.B. asked.

"*A little bit.*"

"*That's what's up*", Knee responded.

"*But yo...if you think she's the bomb wait until I send you some flicks of Alicia.*" I added.

"*Alicia...*"
Knee repeated her name as if it were an exotic cuisine.
"*That's the girl mommy told me about, the one with green eyes?*"
"*Yeah...that's her.*"
"*Green eyes...? What...? She's a red bone...?*"
Knee loved red boned chicks.
"*Nah...she's browned skinned, dimples, pretty smile, real smart.*"
"*Like you care about her brains*", Knee said jokingly.
"*Oh yeah, and she's a Hottentot*", I added.
"*Hottentots, huh?*" Knee asked.
"*Man, Knee has no clue what a Hottentot is*"
J.B. sarcastically replied.
"*Yes I do.*"
"*Ayat. So what's a Hottentot*", J.B. challenged.
"*That's those African women with the ridiculous asses. Shit. Yo Momma is a Hottentot*"
Knee responded in a matter of fact tone. J.B.'s sneer quickly faded.
"*I mean all jokes aside, you know full well Ms. Barnes is holdin' four aces back there.*"
Smiling from ear to ear Knee continued...
"*Man don't look at me like that - you know your daddy doggie styled ya into existence.*"
I couldn't hold it in any longer; betrayal by my own laughter became my latest crime. Knee's nerves of steel never ceased to amaze me. Like a starter pistol J.B.'s face went blank. I knew, at that moment, what demons he was wrestling with. As a kid I used to hate traveling with J.B. and our mother because as we walked men would stare at her large behind or attempt to start a conversation with her. Our mother being the center of attention never bothered me; it was like walking with a celebrity. But it definitely bothered J.B. Perhaps he felt the need to defend her honor or protect her until our father decided to reappear. Whatever the case, the day would never end without J.B. getting into a heated argument with one of our mother's admirers; so I knew J.B. would not allow Knee a free pass. His poker face and

continued silence told me all I needed to know. Amongst brothers no subject was slated taboo - but still... J.B. threw his arm around Knee's shoulders and began smiling. Knee knew something was coming and so he held his grin. *That's right grin and bare it.* I thought. Changing the subject J.B. asked me,

" *Yo Kay, did Knee tell you that he talks in his sleep?* "
"*Nah.*"
"*Yo J.B. stop playin'*", Knee warned.

Knee shrugged J.B.'s arm from around his shoulders, the first visible sign that he was growing increasingly uncomfortable. He knew he couldn't bully J.B. into silence and so he was hoping J.B. would give him a pass. But before mercy could be shown, I threw a log in the flame.

"*Not the dude who said we were doggie styled into existence; you see he ain't givin' up any passes.*"
"*Yes I would. Come on Kay stop playin'.*"

Knee threw a playful jab my way. The jab was his way of trying to pull me to his side. But it was too late.

"*You a hundred percent right. If it was me talking in my sleep, he would've told you as soon as we got on the visiting floor*", J.B. reasoned.

Hearing J.B.'s logic, Knee knew his protest was a lost cause. So he tried a new tactic.

"*Well go 'head then. Make shit up, you know you good for that.*"
"*Sorry buddy but you can't make shit like this up.*"

I could tell that whatever it was, it was hilarious because J.B. paused for effect.

"*Man Kay, dudes came to get me about 1:30 in the morning telling me Knee's talking in his sleep. I get over there and I can't believe what I'm hearing.*"

J.B. paused for the climax.

"*What, what he say?*"
"*I like sprinkles, please put sprinkles on mine.*"
"*Get the fuck outta here!*"

I was in tears.

"*Not big bad Knee talking to Mr. Softee*", J.B. interjected, "*I hope it wasn't Mr. Softee cause the boy was moaning!*"

Knee's face turned beet red. He didn't find this the least bit funny so he just ignored us. I was laughing so hard that tears were falling down my face. I shot a playful jab at Knee and he shot one back not so playful. For the next forty-five minutes our convo took on a life of its own never resting on any subject for too long, except occasionally J.B. and I would try to figure out what *sprinkles* meant in the dream world.

"*Ya just won't let up*", Knee observed.

"*That sounds like a sprinkling good question*", I shot back.

"*I don't sprinkling know what you're talkin' about*", J.B. followed.

And the gut wrenching laughter would begin again. Despite the circumstances, we were still three the hard way. The camaraderie was still pure. Up until that point, I was unable or unwilling to identify the feeling I had been experiencing for the last few months. Being with them…laughing, debating, and laughing some more without the restraint of my Mother's presence crystallized the feeling into a single exotic word - loneliness. I was lonely. This was the first time in my life I had been away from my big brother for more than two weeks.

When we were younger, we used to attend the Fresh Air Fund's sleep-away camp. Our moms always arranged for us to go at different times. Her reasoning was to give us time away from each other to grow as individuals, but this was something beyond our experience. As the visit wound down, we all felt the sadness descend. We had a good time. J.B. and Knee took pictures with the chain on. J.B. and I were even able to get Knee to consider a cop out. Then it was time for me to leave. In retrospect, I truly believe that we were all on the brink of tears. On the bus ride home, a few tears escaped my eyes; I missed my brothers.

Two days later, I received a phone call from J.B.'s on again off again girlfriend *Kiesha*. She told me that J.B. was going to call at 9 p.m. and he needed to talk to me. *Damn!* I planned on taking *Alicia* out to the movies and a hotel afterwards. That phone call threatened to put a crunch in my plans. I ignored J.B.'s request and went out anyway. The following morning, I picked up the phone to the sound of a stream of curses from J.B., berating me for neglecting his request. Well, according to him, it wasn't a request…it was an order. *Some nerve, this big brother shit is clearly over rated.* I remained silent until he finished. After his tirade, he finally told me that a kat from Marcy named *Fizz,* who was on the visit when I was there, immediately identified the chain and whom it belonged to. According to Fizz, the chain had been the property of a character named *Smooth* from Sumner Projects. The same projects Precious lived in. I immediately thought of her. Since the night of the robbery, I avoided her calls and even took the batteries out of my beeper. I knew I would have to call her to smooth things over. Tell her that I went down south with moms or something. Living on the other side of town did not dim Smooth's reputation. He was an ex dope fiend turned big time drug dealer who was known to have a team of hired guns at his disposal at all times. Smooth preferred young shooters because of the leniency they received from the courts if captured. As I learned later in life, young kats tend to question their orders less and believe in codes of honor. Smooth's hired guns were called *Young Gunz* and their efforts were sending ripples throughout the town.

  J.B. advised me to cash the chain in immediately, a conclusion that seemed obvious to me as well. Yet I knew that the damage had already been done. Smooth must have received word about the fiasco at Fulton Mall by now. He would already know my name and the neighborhood I lived in. I again thought of Precious. Once I got back on track with her, she would give me the 411.

  "Yo J.B., I gotta make a call. Call me back!"
  "Kay-Kay! Don't fuck around. Take that chain to the scales!"
  "Yeah, I hear you man. Call back later…ayat?"
  "Ayat."

  I immediately dialed Precious' number. Her little brother answered the phone and said that she was out. I explained to him that I just got back from North Carolina with my Moms and I wanted her to call me when she returned. I hung up the phone and began to ponder my predicament. Slowly, an overwhelming calm began to wash over me. *Fuck Smooth. Fuck the Young Gunz! Fuck it! Christine's son never cowered from any man!* With my Roscoes and bulletproof vest, like so many shorties in the hood, I truly believed I was ready for WAR.

*   *   *

CHAPTER 5
HIGHEST BIDDER

Wednesday - five days since my convo with J.B. - Precious still had not returned my calls. Every time I called, she was not there. I knew she was upset with me for not taking her shopping as promised. I had $500 put away with intentions of taking her once I got in touch with her. I told myself it wasn't love that compelled me to do this; it was strategy. I needed her eyes and ears and $500 was worth it.

About 3 p.m. that same day, I decided to venture out and see what the fellahs were doing. On my block, the corner was the hang out spot and true to form; the fellahs were all out there. I walked up and began giving them dap. Their greetings were reciprocal in enthusiasm. They were drunk, or at least on the verge of it. They were loud, passing around 40 ounces of Olde Gold. I grew up with these dudes. We went to school together and played childhood games such as Round Up, hot peas and butter, football, b-ball, etc. And though sharing these experiences made me a brother in their eyes, I never really felt this way toward them. Knee called them lames and was quick to treat them as such, whereas, J.B. was good friends with most of them. They sent him letters and pictures while he was on Rikers. Nevertheless, I needed to be around some familiar and safe faces. However after about an hour, their behavior started to become annoying. When one of them made a suggestion to go hang out in the park, I declined never understanding how people could allow themselves to get pissy drunk in public like that. *Good riddance!*

An old timer we called *Handbone* was sitting on a milk crate turned on its side at his usual station - the corner; looking at me smiling. Handbone was a Vietnam Vet who after returning from the war found disappointment after disappointment in search of the elusive American Dream. After twelve years of this, he became a bitter man that discovered his peace in a pint of Wild Irish.

"They are about the most silliest Negroes",

Handbone observed ironically referring to the drunks departing his territory.

"*I know*"

Confirming his observation and smiling at him. Handbone was lonely and so was I. We began to talk. This was the first time I ever spoke beyond the superficial with him. His insight was captivating. Looking back, I realize now just how deprived I was not having any type of Father Figure in my life. Eventually Handbone got around to asking me about the chain.

After realizing that selling the chain would make no difference, that the beef would still be on, I decided to keep the chain and let the chips fall where they may.

"*What jewelry store did you rob youngster?*"
I smiled.

"*I robbed a joker, not a store.*"

"*A joker, huh?*"

"*Yeah, like the one Batman and Robin fought*"
I said rhetorically.

"*Oh…so you consider yourself a caped crusader*"

Handbone asked before taking another swig of his Wild Irish. We both began to laugh. Just as quickly as it started the topic changed.

A few minutes later a black Saab with tints sped by. The back window was rolled down a bit and I could see a female's head in the window. I was reminded of Precious. Perhaps I was paranoid, but I felt as though she was checking me out. Just then I decided to try Precious' number again. I excused myself from Handbone and walked a few feet to a pay phone. I dialed her number and after about the tenth ring her brother answered the phone.

Again Precious was not home and I asked if he had let her know that I've been trying to get in touch with her. Indignantly he assured me he had. I hung up, said my farewell to Handbone and began to leave when I noticed the same black Saab, this time going slowly in the same direction it came from the first time it sped down the block. I should have been more alert. Don't ask me why I wasn't. The oddity of seeing this car again only tweaked my curiosity. As the car passed by me the back door flew open violently. That's when my *Spidey Senses* began to tingle. My focus was entirely on the car. I began to reach for my Roscoe, my eyes never leaving the car. At this point the car passed me and was about a half block away. The back door of the car still remained ajar. Something wasn't right.

Only destiny was responsible for my sudden urge to look back. At that moment I understood; the car was nothing but a diversion. The young gun was just about on me. He was young, my age or younger, dark skinned with a gold tooth...he was smiling. His gun was aimed at me...he was smiling. I drew my gat. He fired. So did I. His gun roared like a canon. Mine popped like a firecracker. We both missed. His shots came in rapid succession. Mine weren't as rapid. I was running backward. He was moving toward me...still smiling. I attempted to cut in between two parked cars, trying to get myself into a better position that would provide some cover; when I first felt a searing and then excruciating burn in my neck. I knew I was hit. Another hit literally lifted me off my feet. Oddly I felt no burn.

I couldn't allow myself to stay down; like Ali I got up. He was closing in...still fuckin' smiling. Closing my eyes I fired; another hot missile opened my lids back up. This time the bullet tore through my leg. He reached for the chain hanging temptingly from my neck but missed. I fired again and again. I heard my would be assassin yelp. Soon as I felt the possibility of a victory starting to mount another bullet slammed into me and I landed on the ground...hard. At least I was able to wipe that fuckin' smile off that muthafucka's face. He was out of bullets, holding his shoulder. He began to jog toward the Saab. I squeezed the trigger letting off two more shots before I too found myself out of bullets. Rolling from my back to my stomach then onto my knees, I watched the young gun's retreat.

The black Saab was speeding in reverse, its driver determined to meet its *star performer*. The back door of the car was still open, my would be assassin jumped in. As he did, a female's arm reached out and closed the door. I knew that arm from anywhere. How could I ever forget it - it was attached to a bracelet I stole and gave to - Precious. I was hit. Not physically, but emotionally at this revelation. It felt like another bullet piercing my flesh. I sat down in the middle of the street as the car sped off. I dropped the gun and began searching myself.

Gun smoke blurred my vision, lingering in the air like a pregnant cloud - lighter than gravity but heavy enough to strangulate my breathing I began to panic. Blood was everywhere. My hand was saturated with blood. I was beginning to pass out. I remember Handbone picking up the gun and passing it to somebody…someone unfamiliar. My vision was blurring. Handbone was telling me something, but as hard as I tried I couldn't grasp what he was saying. I fell back, no longer able to sit up. I didn't want to die. *Somebody get my Moms!* Handbone tied something around my leg and applied pressure to the wound at my neck. He was holding my hand the way a Father would. Faintly I heard the sirens or was it demons welcoming a new arrival? I thought of Precious and like any commodity…she simply went to the highest bidder. Then all went black.

*   *   *

Seductively the bracelet caught my eye. It was late January; cold and icy as I carefully wove my way through the slushy street called Canal. I was window-shopping. This was a hobby of mine. I like to stay abreast of all the latest styles, freshest kicks; and the hottest coats. Occasionally I would stop at the jewelry store window, just to peer in and see what they had to offer. Up until that point I never contemplated buying any jewelry from a store. Not when there was so much walking around me daily that I had no problem helping myself.

Yet even through the plexi-glass window, amidst countless other shiny metals, the bracelet and its craftsmanship stood out. I stood there for about five minutes just looking at it - wondering how much a trinket like that would cost. It didn't look heavy, about sixteen pennyweights at best but its design gave it an alluring affect.

Against my window-shopping protocol, I walked into the store. An elderly Oriental man and what I assumed to be his family ran the establishment. There were about seven other consumers in the store besides me, all looking at the various showcases. Most of them were in the back of the store where the diamond section was located. The old man walked up to me and with a mask and tone thinly veiling his hostility asked could he help me. Immediately my blood began to boil. I entered his place of business with the best of intentions - simply wishing to inquire about the price of the bracelet. It was at that moment I knew I was going to liberate the bracelet. Something so exquisite, so beautiful should not be held in captivity by the likes of such an old decrepit man.

I responded calmly,

"Yeah. I'm looking for a little girl's chain for my daughter."

"Ahh...a little girl chain you say?"

"I say."

"Good. Good. Over here."

The old man beckoned me to follow him to a display case far to the right of the one with the bracelet in it.

The door to the store could only be opened electronically by a button behind the cash register. I knew that my patience in this caper was my only option. The entire display was dedicated to little kids and infants. After a lengthy perusal, I decided on a gold ring with a rhinestone in the center. It was small enough to fit an infant. The price tag said $50 but after a brief haggle with the old man, the price was changed to $35. I pulled out the knot of money I had in my front pocket and as expected the old man's entire demeanor changed. No longer was I viewed as a suspect. I now became an honored guest.

After purchasing the ring I pretended to prepare to leave when a tall stocky Oriental dude asked me if I was interested in buying anything else. I smiled my most gullible smile and said...

"No thanks."

I continued to walk toward the door and pretended that something suddenly caught my eye. I stopped and peered over the display case. Both the old man and his son were there in a flash. I pointed to the bracelet and asked how much.

"$750...like to see, like to see?" Reluctantly I agreed. He used his key to open up the display case and gently, as if he wanted to stress its value, lifted the bracelet out of the showcase and handed it carefully to me.

My initial assessment of the bracelet was premature, to say the least. It was beautiful. At its center the bracelet hosted a three dimensional stallion with ruby eyes and white gold chips as its teeth. The horse was blessed with multi-colored wings that extended onto the rest of the bracelet. I pulled up the sleeve of my leather goose and placed it on my wrist. The old man clasped the bracelet shut. He smiled and so did I. We walked over to the mirror, which coincidentally happened to be close to the cash register.

I began making different poses in the mirror, stalling for time. Just then one of the seven customers was preparing to leave, the old man pressed the button and the door opened. I bolted, crashing into a lady as I blasted past her through the door. The old man was caught, I'm sure completely off guard. His son was not and was on my tail. The cold air hit me refreshingly and I knew I was off to the races. I felt something snag on to my coat. I heard my pursuer curse in Chinese. I dared to look. The bracelet though big, was clearly designed for a woman, and so my options were to either sell it or give it away. My moms, would not accept the gift no matter what fabulous tale I spun for her. Precious with the hot and accommodating pussy came to mind. I must be falling for her. Faded into the scenery I looked back and saw the Chinese dude lying flat on his ass. Apparently the slush and ice were too much for his slippers to bear. I also noticed a stress of feathers pouring from the back of my leather goose.

I kept running not daring to stop or slow down. The coat kept pouring out feathers. I knew that as long as I kept the coat on, I would be easy to track. Despite the freezing temperature, I took the coat off and inspected it. Just as I feared, there was a long gash from the right shoulder to the left hip in the back of my coat. He must have used a razor or knife to cause such damage. My $250 coat was ruined. I found the nearest dumpster and threw the coat away.

I was frozen, practically stiff, when I finally made it into a warm train. People looked at me strangely, probably wondering where my coat was. As if in response to their inquisitive stares I directed their gaze to my gleaming wrist as if the jewel provided heat and comfort. I guess I appeared to be another weirdo in a city full of them. And after the initial novelty of my appearance wore off, I, like everything else to these people became invisible.

* * *

CHAPTER 6
CASUALTY

I woke to the sound of different beeping tones and distant voices. Slowly I became aware of my surroundings. Though my vision was blurry, I smelled and heard enough to know that I was in the hospital. So many thoughts raced through my mind. The over ridding thought being...I survived? *I survived!*

Today, so many years later, I marvel at how profound that realization was for me. Very few people know what it feels like to dance with death; to be exposed to the naked pressure; trying to dodge bullets at point blank range; facing the inevitability of those hot invaders searing holes through your flesh; a piercing reminder of how precious life really is.

Yeah I survived, but my victory party was cut short once I realized that my wrist was handcuffed to the bed. I was under arrest? For what - I had no clue. I was doing so much dirt that it could be anything from any number of my adventurous capers. I vaguely recalled Handbone taking my gun, so I quickly ruled out a gun charge. I began to think that I killed the creep during the shoot out. In that case, I would gladly stand before a jury of twelve. About the shooting down by the mall, I knew those kats wouldn't tell. As my pressure began to rise, my heart monitor began beeping faster and louder. The sudden shift in noise caused an elderly nurse to rush into the room. Upon seeing me conscious she smiled.

"*Praise be! You came through so soon after your operation!*" She spoke with a heavy Caribbean accent.

"*Where am I?*" painfully I asked; a reminder that I was shot in the neck.

"*You are in the trauma unit at Kings County Hospital.*"

She asked me to call her Nurse Elaine. She began to ask me routine questions regarding any pain or discomfort I was feeling. I too asked her a series of questions regarding my condition. She did her best to answer most of my questions.

Some of the questions I asked Nurse Elaine, she was stumped for answers...like what I was under arrest for. I did learn that the surgery to extract two bullets lodged in my left thigh, the removal of shell fragments and the repair of my shattered collarbone was successful. I had been hit with two more bullets in the area the police refer to as the *center mass*. This is the kill zone. Fortunately I was wearing the bulletproof vest. *Good old Dave finally came thru for once!* Apparently the vest totally stopped one slug and greatly slowed the other to the point of only leaving a black and blue mark along with a gash on my chest. As I thought about it, I remembered both shots. They were the shots that floored me. I was hit five times and grazed once. After checking my vitals, Nurse Elaine exited the room promising to come right back. As I waited for her return, I began to take a closer look at my medical prison.

The windows had bars on them. Observing the adjacent building through the barred windows of the room I occupied, I could tell I was in one of the top floors. I heard men's voices growing louder by the second. I looked toward my room door knowing with certainty that at any moment the bodies attached to those voices would enter. They did. Two black men dressed in *JC Penney* suits entered the room.

Their faces disfigured in masked only men dedicated to national security could fully appreciate. The chubby one showing his badge spoke first.

"*I am Detective Murray. This is Detective Greene. We are from the Internal Affairs Division of the NYPD. We have a few questions we need answers to; questions that may prove beneficial for you. If you refuse to cooperate we can guarantee that we can make your life a living hell.*"

I just stared at Heckle and Jeckle, wanting to laugh in their faces but deciding it wasn't wise to do so at this point. The skinny magpie with the receding hairline followed up his partner's introduction with...

"*Where did you get the vest?*"

I attempted to speak; pretending that great effort was needed to do so, although I only allowed mumbles to be heard. I was bluffing. Yet for some reason, despite my thespian rendition of the wounded hero, Heckle remained unimpressed. He knew I could talk. I didn't care. I was in acting mode; determined to play my part until the end. Jeckle asked me if I knew that the vest was the property of the NYPD and that it was reported stolen from a police cruiser about a year ago. My eyes radiated surprise. No acting was needed in response to that bit of information. I attempted to speak and after displaying my frustrated attempts, I simply shook my head *no* to convey my answer.

"Stealing from the government is a serious offense young man!"
I pretended to be offended at this accusation.
"Sooner or later you'll talk, all you little punks do."
Heckle was pointing that *Father knows best* finger at me; you know the one they teach those muthafuckas in the Police Academy how to use. He then stormed out of the room. *Bravo!* I thought of his performance.

"Don't mind my partner. He's upset. He knows you didn't rob the cruiser. He doesn't want you to throw away your future trying to protect a bunch of dirty cops. We spoke to your Mother. She's a really sweet woman."

After hearing the word *sweet* in reference to my moms by this pig, his good cop routine fell on deaf ears. *Where was she? Was she here in the hospital?* I needed to see my moms to let her know that her baby survived. Jeckle finally finished his spiel. He told me to think hard about all that he said. He smiled and left. My painkillers were wearing off. *Nurse Elaine…where was Nurse Elaine?*

About two hours later, my mother arrived. Words cannot describe how happy I was to see her. No matter the circumstance, moms' presence always made me feel invincible. I smiled; so did she, until the puddles of tears in her eyes began to swell.

"Boy…what's wrong with you?"
She was exasperated. I tried to laugh it off.
"Ain't nuffin' Ma. I'm ayat."

"No son. You are not all right. You are out of your goddamned mind. You and J.B. will be the death of me. My heart can't take all of this worrying."
She looked at me expecting an answer. What could I say? That when I got home...whenever that would be...that I would walk the straight path? That I would find a job stocking cans or sweeping the floors in a fuckin' supermarket? Somehow I knew she wanted...needed me to lie to her. Similar to the way my Father must've lied before he walked out of our lives. I couldn't. For the second time in one day, I was mute. Not because I didn't want to talk. Rather, any word spoken would hurt her more. I was already too far-gone.

Two weeks shy of my sixteenth birthday and already I knew this was the life I chose. Parents know their children. My silence spoke profound truths to my mother's heart. She began to sob uncontrollably. With my free hand I caressed her hair. She stopped crying long enough to look me in my eye and call me selfish. Was I selfish? Is crime an act of selfishness? Did I think about the effect my decisions were having on my mother? Did I care? I'm sure I would have claimed I did, but did I really? Was my lust for vengeance selfish, because I surely felt it? It's easy for me to sit here eighteen years later and ponder such notions. That day, when my moms said I was selfish, I was clueless to what she really meant.

The following days went by like a blur. Between the doctors, the D.A., my lawyer and the police, I remained busy. Heckle and Jeckle never returned. However, two other uniformed cops arrived and read me my rights. I was under arrest for illegal possession of a bulletproof vest. I mentioned Heckle and Jeckle's visit to my lawyer and my concerns. He got right on top of it and after making a few calls was able to tell me there was some type of investigation underway in the 75th Precinct. Beyond this, my attorney could get no more information.

I spent my sixteenth birthday in the hospital. The officer assigned to guard my room allowed me to celebrate the day free of handcuffs. My mother, Alicia and Nurse Elaine sang *Happy Birthday* to me and surprised me with an ice cream cake. Due to the wounds in my leg, I was immobile, so I sat up in bed and enjoyed the day. It was a good day. The doctor told me that I would have a scar on my neck directly above my collarbone from the bullet wound. Other than that I would be fine.

A month later I was taken to central booking and then to my surprise, I was shipped to Rikers Island. I knew this was a mistake. The police who drove me to Rikers Island also knew it was a mistake because I was fifteen at the time of my arrest. I was supposed to be taken to a detention center for juveniles called *Spofford*. Instead they decided to house me with the big boys.

Physically I was extremely weak. When I was released from the hospital, I discovered that I lost twenty-three pounds. I entered the prison system weighing only 131 pounds. Despite the mistake I was ecstatic that I was being sent to Rikers. J.B. and Knee were there and in a few hours I was destined to once more be amongst them.

*   *   *

CHAPTER 7
ADOLESCENTS AT WAR

I was driven to C-74, the adolescent building on Rikers Island. The cold blue on white walls of the receiving room caught my attention first, then the noise. 9 p.m. for the receiving room was still rush hour. This was the place where all the prisoners going to and coming from court were processed. Eight large holding cells made up the slave quarters on this particular plantation; a place where upon immediate entry an oppressive and hopeless feeling descends.

As I was being escorted past the cells I saw countless unrecognizable faces, all pressed against the cold steel bars. All eyes were on me; wanting to get a good look at the new jack. Sizing me up, checking out my gear, my sneakers, and my walk; if I appeared afraid, would I be easy prey - all these thoughts I registered in their stares.

Determined to pass any test, I stared back - reflecting in my eyes the hostility I saw in theirs. My captors beckoned me to turn; I did. Yet I refused to break the stare. The officer had to tell me, a couple of times, to look straight ahead, only then were the optical combats completed. There were no winners only a promise of a future rendezvous.

I was escorted down a long gloomy blue corridor until finally being directed into a small brightly lit orange room. The word *INTAKE*, lettered in black was the only other color on the wall. At the time I had no clue that the colors of any particular prison wall had a specific purpose. The fact that certain colors can play a role in reducing or enhancing a desired mood was a foreign and far too advanced notion for me at that time. All I saw, if anything, was a bad paint job. Later I learned that the gloomy blue paint was designed to foster a sense of hopelessness and despair, while bright orange was designed to create a feeling of being overwhelmed. Both sensations I felt but failed to comprehend its cause.

The Intake Room held three holding cells. I was placed into one occupied by two other dudes. By the look of apprehension on their faces, I knew that this was their first time on the Island. At first we engaged in small talk. After a couple of minutes I learned that Ice and Jabbar, co-defendants out of East New York, were the newest celebrities in the hood. Just three days prior, they robbed Raquel Welch for a ton of jewelry.

The robbery was in all the major newspapers and on the news. Someone dropped a dime anticipating a reward, yet despite their apprehension the jewelry remained missing. I enjoyed hearing about the heist and their audacity triggered my sincere admiration. About an hour later we were escorted out of the cell to begin the Intake Process. After being stripped, searched, fingerprinted and finally examined by a nurse, we were each provided a *set up* which consisted of toiletries and two bed sheets rolled up inside a blanket. We were then taken to the housing unit for new inmates. The housing unit was nicknamed the *New Jack House*.

It was dark when we walked into the dormitory style unit. Fifty beds spread out before us with only a few beds empty. Most of the prisoners were asleep, but a few were still awake - staring. We were escorted to empty beds and then left to fend for ourselves. I didn't even attempt to unpack or make up the bed. After about an hour of just simply sitting on the edge of the bed waiting for a confrontation to happen that didn't, I decided to relax. Placing the roll up at the head of the bed it became my unofficial pillow. Still fully waiting for my first example to emerge, as usual, I began to daydream about my favorite subject: the obliteration of Smooth, his shooter and Precious.

*   *   *

'84 Easter, Coney Island...Knee and I were coming off the boardwalk heading toward an amusement park ride called The Hell Hole when I spotted her. She was standing slightly apart from a crowd of loud-mouthed chicks – daydreaming. Her slender waist and high bubble butt threw my senses into a fog. Even at fourteen I was a sucker for a shapely ass. Her almond

shaped brown eyes were only a shade lighter than her deep chocolate complexion; a compliment of contrast, giving her an untamed exotic look. After a rough introduction I learned that her name was...Precious.

Knee and I were in the midst of chasing paper and so I wasn't able to holla at her for too long. I could tell she was feeling me by the tone of her conversation. Like sugar and water our chemistry became one. Knee grew impatient...

"Hey Casanova...Casanova!"

"Your brother...?"

"Yeah...the crazy one."

Even from ten feet away I could see Knee's comical expression as he called me. I couldn't help but laugh. Precious laughed too. We exchanged info and I promised her that I would call. For an entire week her beauty remained the fixture of my desires. I could hold out no longer and finally dialed her up. Our relationship blossomed so fast that in no time we became inseparable.

Precious believed me to be her age. She was 16...two years my senior. Well actually 20 months my senior but who's counting. Her mother was a crack head in the worst way and Precious found herself thrust into the position of being the woman of the house. She took good care of herself and her two younger siblings making sure they did their homework and ironed their clothes before going outside to play. Summertime found her hard at work in the local Pathmark saving her money for the upcoming school year. Precious began talking about us getting an apartment together when we finished high school. I played along with the fantasizing – all the while remaining fully focused on the task at hand – securing a couple of nuts.

Most chicks growing up in the concrete jungle want a man who's willing to protect and defend their honor. Precious, I suppose was no different. It began as a trivial conversation, in her bed, naked under the sheets. She was telling me about the jealous girls in her school and how one chick in particular would go out of her way to bump and spit verbal venom at Precious trying to provoke some kind of a confrontation.

The events Precious detailed were beginning to sound more like a mini drama, I feigned interest. I wasn't with all the pillow talk, stick and move was my theme, but Precious had the uncanny ability to draw you into her world, however dark and illogical it may be. I recall saying to myself that Precious was a punk and that she wasn't as tough as she pretended. Finally, I asked her why she didn't just punch the chick in the mouth, expecting my question to put a quick demise to the frivolous conversation. But as I would stubbornly learn, when it came to Precious, everything she did was methodical. All along she had been leading me, the way any master storyteller could, prodding me to enter her world – daring me to ask the one question that appeared so obvious. Her eyes flooded with pools of water as she began telling me about the big bad wolf.

His name was Kev, the unofficial tough guy of Sarah J. Hale High School in Brooklyn. It was his girlfriend with whom Precious was having difficulties with. Kev had indirectly threatened Precious away from fighting the girl. Of course Precious forgot to mention a couple of minor details, like having a yearlong relationship with Kev before being dumped by him for the chick Precious now had problems with. With such limited information it is no wonder I came to the conclusion that Kev was a sucka muthafucka who needed to be dealt with.

I waited 'til the following Friday afternoon when I knew that the block surrounding the school would be packed with kids hanging out and cutting classes. Fridays were also the days when kids who didn't even attend the school would show up to hang out. I brought along my trusty .25 automatic and two of my homeys, just in case shit began looking iffy.

As we approached the school all eyes fell on me. As expected the street was crowded with kids sitting and leaning on parked cars. It was obvious that we came there for trouble and some of their stares suggested that perhaps they were ready.

Precious, anticipating my arrival emerged from a cluster of clucking chicks to give me a big hug and kiss. The display of affection was obviously theatrical, intended to let the onlookers know who we were because neither one of us was big on kissing. I spoke to Precious loud enough for all in the immediate vicinity to hear.

"Where's this dude Kev?"

"He's right over there."

Precious pointed toward a large crowd of people at the end of the block. As we made our way toward Kev, the small groups of guys and girls began to follow, an entourage of spectators preparing to witness a lively showdown.

Walking head first into the unknown, not knowing what to expect caused an endless flurry of butterflies to zip around inside my stomach. I kept telling myself, Kay...don't shoot nobody over a chick. There's no props in some sucka shit like that. Somehow a warning of our approach made it to Kev or maybe seeing Precious approaching and knowing her far better than I, was enough evidence for him to expect trouble.

Courageously he walked toward us, anger emanating from his eyes. His facial expression was a mask of pure disgust directed toward - Precious. With his focus on her, I was able to size up my opponent; a high yellow boy, tall and lanky about 6'2" with beady eyes. He was sporting a blue suede front jacket with about eight skinny gold chains dangling from his long neck. One glance at my two companions confirmed my suspicion that this confrontation was about to turn into a robbery.

"Precious...what the fuck you bring these dudes up to my school for? I told your silly ass I don't want to have anything to do with you."

Precious cut him off quickly realizing that she already allowed him to say far too much. Craftily Precious seized control of the argument...

"So you gonna smack me huh? You gonna break my neck if I fight this bitch?"

She was pointing at a chinky-eyed beauty whose name was April – advertised by the gold name buckle that helped accentuate her curvy hips. At least he dumped her for something just as beautiful. Kev looked baffled like he had no clue what she was talking about.

"Fuck you wanna fight somebody who doesn't want to fight you? ...Stupid bitch!"

Kev was yelling at Precious – his first mistake.

"Yo dude...who the fuck you calling a bitch", I asked, challenging him to make another mistake – he did. For the first time Kev looked at me. I could read his eyes. He was wondering who the fuck I was.

"Fuck is you? ...her little brother or something? Shorty go play somewhere. Grown folks are talking."

I heard the crowd snigger in amusement. Out of all the nerves Kev could've chose – he hit the most sensitive one. I was a little dude, who harbored a gigantic Napoleon Complex. My gun was in my hand before my mind registered its presence. Kev's eyes grew wide; his hands went up pleadingly, the collective gasp from the crowd energizing me. The circle around us widened. People were preparing to run at the sound of the first gunshot.

"Grown folks...? Grown folks...? You faggot muthafucka! You know who the fuck I am?"

I was losing control fast. My finger was flirting dangerously with the trigger, just waiting for the command. Not fully realizing his mistake, Kev stuck his foot in his mouth further.

"Yo shorty...I don't want no probs."

"Shorty? Shorty!"

I was yelling moving in for the kill, fire raging inside of me, growing stronger with every step forward. A hand caught my shoulder, calmly a voice whispered in my ear...

"Not over a broad. Not over a broad."

HONOR AMONGST THIEVES

The voice of reason belonged to my man Young God – one of my two companions. His logic brought me back to sanity.

"Muthafucka...run those chains, those fuckin' rings and the suede front."

The confrontation was now a robbery. Kev wasn't stupid. He immediately complied and so did his man. While both Kev and his man were stripping...

"You wanna fight this bitch?" I asked.

It was like unleashing a greyhound. Precious crouched low and charged. Her and April locked horns with a fury. It was obvious that the hate between them was mutual. April was just as pretty as Precious but not as shapely. She had a delicate look to her – the kind of look girls have when they are only used to looking pretty – and that's where Precious had the edge. She wasn't just pretty, she was tough.

The fight looked even for all of thirty seconds before Precious found herself on top of the girl pummeling her head into the concrete. Like any true thief I heard the faint wail of sirens growing louder by the second. It was time to boogie...

"Precious...let's go!"

She didn't respond. As I grabbed her off the girl Precious' foot connected with April's already bloody face. I remember thinking; damn...she might not be pretty anymore. We were off to the races, all four of us...my two goons, me and Precious.

The next morning, Precious was arrested at her crib for the assault. April's mother was pressing charges. Two nights later Precious was released on her own recognizance. Precious wanted to go get 'the bitch' that very night for ratting. Her plan was to throw bleach in the poor girl's face when she opened her front door. I laughed it off and tried talking her out of it but Precious refused to budge.

"C'mon Precious, stop playing. That shit ain't worth it."

"Fuck that bitch. She pop all that shit, get her ass beat, and then run to the cops? I should've really made that bitch ugly."

For a split second I saw something in her eyes that sent a chill down my spine. I looked at my lap and wrote it off. Distracted by Precious pacing back and forth. All that fat ass in those Jordache jeans was enough to have any man's undivided attention. I stood up and grabbed a handful of her box braids. I began kissing and sucking on her neck.

Let the game began.

"Stop playin' Ka-" I stuck my tongue in her mouth. She kept twisting her face but I still had a hand full of braids.

"You play too much. Stop!"

I grabbed her ass with my free hand and kept kissing all over her neck and shoulders, all the while tightening my grip on her hair.

"Let go of my hair Ka-"

I pulled her closer and shoved my tongue back in her mouth. This time with a force she readily accepted. Although she kept twitching her body like she wanted me to let her go, I remained in control. I turned her around so her back was to me. I continued to kiss and suck on her neck and play with her titties through her blouse. When I unbuttoned her jeans and slid my hands down her pants, I found her pussy dripping wet. Game Over.

I sat back down on the bed with Precious standing in front of me. As she started to unbutton her blouse I took off my shirt. She was wearing a yellow bra with a little flower in the front. She took off the bra, and I swear I never get used to seeing those perfect titties.

Her nipples were a perfect circle, which stood up like little soldiers when I flicked my tongue across them. She wiggled out of her Jordache jeans, and at the sight of all that soft flesh protruding out of her flower printed panties, made my dick harder than frozen concrete.

I guess she saw it too, because she lunged straight for it. Opening up my belt and jeans in one fluid motion. I rose up so she could pull my pants down and off. When she grabbed my dick she looked at me with this lustful look in her eyes, and devoured me like her life depended on it. I know grown women who can't give head like that. I took up another hand full of braids, and enjoyed the ride.

She started at the head making circles with her tongue, her mouth, so warm and soft relaxed me completely. Then she deep throated me in one long gulp. I could feel her cheek muscles tightening around my joint like her pussy does when I make her cum. She probably could've blessed me all day but I just couldn't take anymore. I pulled her up off the floor and onto the bed.

I laid down on top of her and started kissing on her neck while fingering her pussy. Precious was so wet; I couldn't wait to slide up in her. She let out a soft moan and the sound of it went straight to the tip of my dick. I proceeded to lick and kiss her all over her body down to her belly button. Kissing between her thighs and brushing past her lips drew her into a frenzy.

Finally I put my tongue on her clit and licked it slowly, savoring her taste. She put her hand on the back of my head to keep me from moving. She had nothing to worry about. I sucked and licked on her pussy for what seemed like forever. Every time I made her cum, it just made me want to keep going.

"Kay, put it in me."

Music to my ears.

"Please put it in me"

I got on my knees, spread her legs and went right up in her. She fit like a glove around my dick. Giving her deep, long strokes I wanted her to feel every inch of me. Precious wrapped her legs around my waist to allow me full penetration and no lie; I tried to reach her lungs. Feeling her pussy muscles throbbing around me was driving a dude crazy. So, before I splashed off, I needed to stop.

"Turn that ass over."

I demanded, loving her submissiveness when it came to sex. On her knees with all that ass in the air, I dove right in.

Tearing that pussy to shreds. The more she moaned, the harder I pounded. When she tried to run I held her by the waist and showed no mercy. Damn she was so wet and warm I just stopped fighting with myself and let off the nut heard 'round the world right up in her. Her pussy squeezed out what ever I had to give. When it was all over we were both drained and sticky. I rolled over and smacked her on the ass.

"Leave that girl alone."

"I ain't even thinkin' 'bout that chick."

It wasn't until I buried myself deep inside of her that she finally let go of the revenge notion; at least for that night. I always had that affect on her...until now. So what happened?

*   *   *

The yell of... *"On the count!"*...woke me. It was early morning.

It took three days for me to get in the swing of the prison's schedule. I was slated to remain in the New Jack House for at least seven days before I would be allowed into general population; however I was able to see J.B. every evening in the Law Library where he worked as a clerk. I was surprised at how adept J.B. had become in understanding and interpreting the law. Everybody, it seemed, came to him for legal advice. In this arena, J.B. was clearly in his element. Nonetheless, time was set aside for us to kick it and strategize. Knee was still in isolation. There were quite a few dudes in the building I knew, mostly from my hood. They would all play the Law Library bringing food and cosmetics for their fellow P.O.W. Everyone wanted to know about the drama with Smooth, the shooting and the set up. I learned that the shooter was a kid out of Tompkins Projects ironically called *Smiley*.

Besides seeing J.B., I was also extremely happy to see my man Sha. Sha and I attended the same JHS. He was a year older and a great deal bigger. Sha, even as a kid, was a big muthafucka standing at about 6'2" and weighing well over 200

HONOR AMONGST THIEVES

lbs. He was also the biggest adolescent in the building. Back when we were in school together I used to take Sha on robbery missions with me using his size as a scare tactic.

Like Knee, Sha's jail reputation transcended the walls, *ringing bells* in the streets. J.B. spoke to me about him one day on a visit, but I had no idea it was my school buddy he was referring to. Sha was from Brownsville. In '85 and '86 the Brownsville Kats ran the building. Naturally, there were warriors from every neighborhood and borough who were able to hold their own; but by sheer numbers, the unity exhibited amongst them and their skills in fighting made Brownsville's *never ran never will* - formidable.

Big Sha, which he was now referred to was the leader of the pack. He had been in jail for five months fighting a murder beef. J.B. had begun helping Sha prepare a defense for trial. They became good friends without realizing that I was one of two links between them; Knee being the other.

Knee and Sha couldn't stand one another! What happened was when Sha first went to general population he landed in *Mod 9*, a housing unit run by Knee. Knee hated Brownsville dudes and would limit their phone calls to six minutes. When Sha's six minutes became eight minutes, Knee sent his loyal soldier, *Benetton* to hang up the phone on Sha. With one punch Benetton was put to sleep. Sha, still holding the phone receiver in his hand, unplugged the phone and walked to the back of the housing unit demanding to know whose phone it was. Having secured his razor, Knee spoke up…

"Yo shorty! Where you going with my jack?"

This is the type of humor Knee had even when the pressure was on. Knee was only 5'9", 170 lbs., at least five inches shorter and 40 lbs. lighter; yet he still referred to Sha as shorty.

Seeing the razor in Knee's hand, Sha panicked and threw the phone receiver hitting Knee. Sha ran toward the front of the housing unit and to what he must have thought was the safety of the officers' bubble. More than twenty dudes with broomsticks, mop ringers and razors were in hot pursuit. Sha made it to the front of the housing unit but had to wait for the officers to let him out. With his back to the door he began fiercely cursing, kicking and spitting.

Having seen first hand what one punch from Sha could do, the wolf pack held their distance, content with swinging their weapons at Sha, that is - except Knee. He was determined to cut the *big nigga* for violating. With Sha swinging his fists, and Knee swinging the razor, both became locked in a battle that would go down in 4 building history. Somehow, Knee dropped the razor and was forced to fight Sha head up.

According to everyone who witnessed the fight, including the C.Os, the fight was a classic; one that was still being talked about in the gloomy halls of the Island as if it just occurred yesterday. It became one of those events where prisoners used to keep track of time. Things happen either *before the fight* or *after the fight*.

Knee with his quick hands and 52 Defense was able to hang with the slower but extremely hard-hitting Sha. It was said that Sha hit Knee with some seriously hard shots, the kind that made the spectators cringe. Twice Knee went down hard and another time he buckled under the force of Sha's blows. But Knee was a warrior and warriors never quit. For every shot Sha was able to deliver Knee delivered three, finally landing one punch that put Sha on his ass. Quickly Sha recovered and that's when everyone agreed that the fight really began. Both gladiators grudgingly grew respectful of one another, realizing that a lot more was at stake than just a black eye or bloody nose. As far as jail house politics went, this fight was like the presidential election. None of the onlookers had any interest in breaking up the fight. They fought until fatigue took over; both surrendering stubbornly to exhaustion. Huffing and puffing they simply stared at each other.

At the conclusion, both men had faces that resembled Mr. Marshmallow. After being taken to the infirmary and cleared of any serious injuries, Knee was allowed to return to the housing unit while Sha was placed in another. It's been my experience that when two men fight like that they eventually become the very best of friends. This was not the case. While they both held great respect for each other's capabilities, the friendship never materialized. Perhaps Knee, resented that Sha made a name for himself at his expense; that Sha was four years younger, or perhaps it was simply what followed next.

Throughout the following months, everyone with the exception of Knee; that was housed in Mod 9 felt the wrath of Sha. He caught some of the guys going to court, some coming off visits or going to sick call or the Law Library - it didn't matter. Wherever he found them he would beat, humiliate and rob them. He wouldn't stop until they begged...

"Please Big Sha. Please have mercy on me."

Yeah...when I heard it I laughed too. Benetton succeeded in cutting Sha across his cheek before being knocked out, robbed for his sneakers, and urinated on. From that day on Benetton was known as *Pissy B*. Sha's reputation began to transcend Knee's and so Knee began to turn up the heat as well. Targeting Sha's affiliates, Knee robbed and cut a bunch of them. A major schism developed in the 4 building behind these two strong personalities. Reputations were won and lost in the ongoing drama. Finally after three months of daily drama a truce was called. A meeting was set up between all the recognized steppers in the building with the only no show being the kats in the bing of which Knee was once again a part of. J.B. was instrumental in the whole peace process. Most guys respected J.B. for being a real muthafucka and although he and Knee were the best of friends, J.B. was able to separate himself from most of Knee's drama. Nevertheless, at the end of the day when shit hit the fan, J.B. would be at Knee's side.

Having great respect for J.B., Big Sha understood that having beef with Knee would eventually extend to J.B. and so he agreed to squash the beef. Of course, Knee was much more stubborn about agreeing to a truce and only after he robbed one more Brownville kat did he finally agree. From that point on whenever Sha and Knee found themselves in the same vicinity, they both would act as if the other didn't exist. Of course that was the most J.B. could have expected, but now that I was in the building even that wasn't good enough. Knee's hatred for Brownsville kats bordered on psychopathic...

*   *   *

One day back in '83, Knee decided to go, by himself, to a jam in the Brownsville Houses. The jam was packed with people partying. He was leaning on a fence, sipping a wine cooler, enjoying the sounds, when suddenly and unexpectedly cold steel was being pressed against Knee's cheek. While everyone looked on, Knee was ordered to hand over his black fur Kangol hat, black with gold trim Gazelle frames, black suede bubble gum soled Wallabee shoes and after a thorough pat down, his wallet and .25 automatic was also located and liberated. As any good stick up kid knows, the key to being successful lies in the element of surprise – we called it catching the drop. Knee realized that his bandit had the drop on him and wisely decided not to resist.

What made Knee's compliance less difficult was when he looked at the man holding the shotgun. Immediately, Knee knew that resistance spelled death, for out of all the stick up artists in the world it was Knee's lucky day that the worst of the worst chose him. The guy gripping the 12 gauge was none other than Kill 'em Dead himself. Word. Kill 'em Dead or K.D. was an old timer pushing close to forty. Once the war chaplain for the Tomahawks, his reputation of daring exploits and cold-blooded murders spanned two decades.

In the mid-sixties and early seventies the Tomahawks were the biggest gang in the borough of Brooklyn. Though their chapters could be found all throughout Brooklyn, their base was in the projects of Brownsville. As the erosion caused by heroin took its toll on an unsuspecting community, the Tomahawks slowly lost its appeal. Most of its members found themselves in prison doing long stretches, or scratching and nodding in a state

HONOR AMONGST THIEVES

of euphoric bliss, in hallways and alleyways from the heroin they injected daily into their veins. The fate that befell the Tomahawks hadn't escaped K.D.

After serving a nine year prison stint, he returned to his old stomping grounds – a dope fiend with not a monkey but a gorilla on his back. In order to support the gorilla, K.D. turned to stick ups. With absolutely no fear of reprisals, K.D. simply did what he wanted. And according to the streets, he had no problem robbing a live body or a freshly made corpse – especially a corpse of his own creation.

Kill 'em Dead had a burn mark above his right eye that made his eye lid droop. Such a distinguishing scar, where upon seeing it without ever having seen it before, you knew exactly who he was, I believe this is why Knee gave up without a fight. He understood that the predator holding the instrument of death was none other than death himself. Needless to say, the robbery was a crushing blow to Knee's ego; a blow made all the more humiliating because Knee was a stick up kid himself who was forced to take a long walk back to the train station wearing nothing on his feet except a pair of argyle socks.

For three weeks straight Knee went back to the "Ville" looking for Kill 'em Dead but never caught up to him. Eventually Knee's anger subsided but not his humiliation. Knee felt that someone in the crowd had set him up and thus his animosity toward anything Brownsville – was born. Regardless of the fact that K.D. was hated and feared in the 'ville as well, such minor details were overlooked by knee..

As for K.D., not too long after he caught Knee sleeping was his own fate sealed. K.D. decided to take his one man show on the road and Crown Heights was the neighborhood of choice. After making his presence known with a string of brazen robberies, a couple of hustlers throughout the hood decided it was in their best interests to pool their resources and place a $5000 marker on his head. At the mere sight of K.D. shots would be fired from kats eager to cash in on the five grand marker. For K.D. it was obviously all a game. Like hide and seek, K.D. would materialize out of nowhere, terrorize the local hustlers and then disappear.

There were many close calls where it seemed K.D. was finally a goner but somehow he found a way to get away. Like the time when a handful of gunmen chased him onto a roof forcing him to make a daring jump from one roof to the next. A jump that none of his pursuers were foolish enough to follow. Many speculated that his safe haven was somewhere in the 'ville. But that wasn't the case, for after seeing the unity of the hustlers and gunmen in Crown Heights, the Brownsville hustlers also placed a five grand marker on K.D's head.

The lucky recipient of the Kill 'em Dead sweepstakes went to a former Tomahawk named Jitterbug. Jitter was living and hustling at the other end of the borough in the projects of Coney Island. One day while driving down Mermaid Avenue, he spotted K.D. walking next to a pregnant woman carrying a bag of groceries. Jitter stopped the car, jumped out and crept up on the creep artist himself.

Word is that the first bullet tore through K.D's back with a force that spun him around like a carousel to face his assailant. K.D. dropped his groceries, a container of milk exploding upon impact. A second shot, a head shot, stopped him from reaching for his gun. K.D. met the asphalt face first, oblivious to his companion's scream. He was probably a goner at this point but Jitterbug left no chance for a potential resurrection. He dumped seven more lava shots to the head ensuring that Kill 'em Dead was finally killed dead. Jitterbug's actions had very little to do with the $10,000 bounty. It was personal; a reason only known to other Tomahawks, a secret – a secret that was sealed in blood.

There were only about 100 people watching and so it goes without saying that to this very day K.D's death remains an unsolved mystery. But the streets know – it always does. That night, countless flares of gunshots momentarily lifted the canopy of night in every hood. On every block, shots were fired in the *air saluting the passing of a warrior. With his death, K.D's transgressions were forgotten. All that remained was his name. In time, like Billy the Kid and Al Capone, Kill 'em Dead would make the smooth transition from villain to hero – immortalized forever in hood folklore.*

*   *   *

CHAPTER 8
LIVE WIRE

The seventh day on the Island arrived and I was moved to 4 Main, *The House of Pain*. Not all housing units had graphic names such as this; only the live ones. Most new jacks were terrified of going straight to the house of pain. Unlike the dormitory style living that the Mods provided, 4 Main was a cell block with each prisoner having his own cell. 4 Main was Big Sha's domain; he made moves to get me to his house.

Walking past the open cells I couldn't help comparing those who were living comfortably to those barely living. Some cells had extra furniture, lockers and chairs draped with big colorful beach towels. Bed sheets and towels decked out methodically, covering all the furniture in such a way as to make the cell appear to be the color of the towels. Besides the towels, there were other signs of affluence associated with being a *live wire*. Bodega displays, showcasing the amount of cosmetics and cigarettes sitting on top of their lockers set in pyramid style shrines. Some cells had well over fifty bars of soap.

Then there was the foot wear we called kicks: Jordans, shell tops and soccer Adidas, Nike, Bally shoes and in one or two cells Gucci sneakers stuck out temptingly from under their beds. Most of these cells possessed seven or eight pairs. They were not gifts sent from loved ones. These trinkets were the spoils of daring exploits; liberated at the point of a knife, razor or other persuasive tactics. Hunters who enjoyed showing off their kills; the kicks were trophies of status for the live wire.

There were other cells-Spartan, practically bare; not by choice but by cowardice. These cells belonged to the prey and not the predator; democracy at its finest. The funny thing was that a lot of these dudes had predatory reps on the street. In the hood they were viewed as gangsters but in prison these illusions were shattered. I was assigned to #12 cell at the back of the hall. Big Sha's cell turned out to be #13; the last cell on the gallery and my next door neighbor. As I approached my cell, Sha emerged from his smiling.

"Main man, I told you I would get you over here.
Main man* was the nickname Sha began calling me. For Sha, I was the closest he had to family in this environment. Most of the guys in the building, even the steppers, were borderline terrified of him. Some masked their fears better than others, but to a discernable eye it was there. To me, Big Sha was just Sha. A big doofus of sorts and since I saw past the image his reputation created, it was easy for Sha to be himself around me. We both stepped into my cell and I immediately began unpacking. Still smiling, Sha began giving me the run down.
"Main man, don't sweat nuffin'. This is my crib. I already let these kats know what time it is with you, so if any of them step out of line..." I interrupted, *"I'll handle them."*
Sha was my dude but I understood that I had to stand on my own two feet. I wasn't the type to sit back and live off of Knee, J.B. or Sha. He understood my sentiments and in truth expected none other. I asked him about the phone situation, what slots was fair game.
Controlling the phones or jack, as we called it on Rikers back in those days, was the ultimate status symbol. Many men's blood was shed over something as trivial as the phone. For the phone provided access to a world left behind; as well as maintaining the myth that despite being locked up the live wire was still in control. Controlling their immediate surroundings as if it were the streets they once roamed.
In every house one or two dudes controlled the phones. A person with no props might get lucky and use the phone for six minutes a day; during *crab time*. In some houses six minutes a week was considered generous. The more props obtained the more time on the jack allowed. Some guys had fifteen minutes others thirty, but by 6 p.m. every night only the live wires touched the phone. There were units where so many steppers lived together that all had thirty minutes a piece from 6 p.m. to 11 p.m. In 4 Main, Sha controlled both the north and south side phones. He would use the south side phone from 6 p.m. to 8:30 p.m. and then get on the north side phone from 9 p.m. to 11 p.m.

The rest of the time was fair game and so the strongest took what their hand called for.

After Sha ran down the phone situation, I told him that I was going to take the 9:30 p.m. to click time on the south side. He told me that three dudes divided the time: Trey, Baby Grand and Mike. Mike and Baby Grand were from Webster Projects in the Bronx while Trey was out of Bed-Stuy, Smooth's stomping grounds. This fact alone made me extremely uncomfortable because Smooth was viewed as a God in Bed-Stuy and Trey could easily attempt to score points with Smooth by shedding my blood. His presence was just too close for comfort and so I decided Trey would be the example.

That night, Sha took me over to the south side and introduced me to the three amigos. Baby Grand and Mike instantly sensed something was up and their defensive postures revealed as much. Trey on the other hand was pretending too hard to act naïve, so I asked him straight up…

"*What's up with Smooth and Smiley?*"

"*What Smooth*",

clearly caught off guard by my bluntness.

"*Smooth from Sumner, Smiley from Tompkins.*"

"*Oh…I DON'T really know, ya heard?*"

"*Word…well do me a favor and give 'em this…*"

I swung hard and fast, my hand gripped the razor as I sliced down his face from forehead to lip like a knife slicing through butter. It took a second for it to register. As soon as it did he swung on me, foolishly trying to grab me, figuring because of my size I would be easy to man handle. I moved quickly, slipping out of his grip easily. Each time I slipped I cut. He began leaking from a handful of different wounds; his courage, like his blood, slowly but surely began to drain. He backed up and was about to make a dash for some type of weapon when Sha blind-sided him with a punch to the head. Trey went down hard.

"*Don't even think about it!*"

Trey lay on the floor utterly defeated. I told him to go to the police bubble and let them know he couldn't live there any more.

"*Oh…and make sure you tell Smooth I'm coming.*"

He glanced at me. In that brief second I saw the confirmation and recognition in his eyes I suspected all along. Quickly, Sha and I made our way back to the north side. The police knew what time it was but as long as Trey didn't snitch they didn't care.

Later that night, after the police escorted Trey and his belongings out of the cell block; after they read us the riot act and threatened to start making some changes; after the captain came by to make his routine inspection, Baby Grand, Mike and I sat down and discussed the phone situation. Sha agreed to give up his use of the south side phone from 6 p.m. to 8:30 p.m. I decided that I was going to take the 7 p.m. to 9 p.m. on the phone, leaving them to split the 9 p.m. to 11 p.m. slot time. Reluctantly they agreed. I knew that their agreement had more to do with Sha, J.B. and Knee than it did me, but there was nothing I could do to remedy that.

Physically I was a little dude and so it was going to take a lot more than a cutting to establish myself on my own merit. C-74 was NYC's gladiator school. Back then it was the place where warriors were polished or broken. My cutting Trey simply meant that my rights of passage had officially begun.

Within a day word spread throughout the building of my frontal attack and once again all eyes were on me. Trey was moved to 3-Lower on the other side of the building. He went to a house ran by a kat named Jah-Loyal. Originally from the Bronx, Jah was living and getting money in Harlem. He was one of the few kats in the building who didn't give a fuck about Knee, Sha or the McDuffy Brothers; two gangstas out of the Bronx who were holding down 2-Main. At twenty-one, Jah was the only truly *rich nigga* in the building. He was a part of a drug crew in Harlem known as PCP, or Purple City Posse.

They had control of a twenty block radius that included two housing projects and a small park, selling every drug under the sun. The leader was a guy by the name of *Bad* who was Jah's older brother and this made Jah the heir apparent to the throne. Unfortunately, for the past eight months Jah was being held in jail without bail for killing a rival in front of countless people during a neighborhood basketball game. To make matters worse, five days later when the police surrounded Jah in his customized BMW, they found a kilo of coke in his trunk.

In jail Jah's money, access to drugs and street reputation placed him in a unique position. Jah was the guy all the gangstas wanted to impress. If Jah decided to pass on a good word to his brother about a person, there would be a lucrative job waiting for them when they made it home. Jah was a master at dangling this carrot; this hope of a better life in the face of his believers. Like the preacher who promises a better life in the afterlife, Jah's promise was just as believable. With his money he was able to afford an army of loyal soldiers from all boroughs that moved at his whim. Through them Jah flooded the jail with weed, coke and dope. While Knee, Sha and the McDuffy's remained the champions of physical force in the building, Jah was unquestionably the God Father. It was Jah who gave Trey sanctuary. Adding one more soldier to his vastly growing army was nothing to him. Yet Trey would become the straw that would break the camel's back. For in the months and years to come Jah would live to regret taking Trey into his fold.

Alicia was my only visitor, besides my mother. She became my light inside a dark tunnel, my breath of fresh air, my woman. Being incarcerated, isolated from your loved ones, forces you to begin to really appreciate their presence in your life. While I was out on the streets I showed Alicia just enough interest and affection to get the pussy when I wanted it. But in prison I began to cherish her company, her voice, and her laughter. I looked forward to receiving mail from her and when I didn't I would literally go into stress mode.

For Alicia, my incarceration, allowed her the opportunity to stake her claim. Every letter, every visit, was for her an investment in our future. Our visits were laced with promises of future bliss, of settling down and having a family. Though conflicted, I went along with the fantasizing. Part of me was committed to the grind. I still had among other things, revenge in my heart and mind. I still was committed to the paper chase, the prop hunt, the adrenaline rush and excitement of the game. Addictions, the kind Alicia could never understand. And so I hid it with a smile and enjoyed our dreaming.

Knee's ex-girl gave birth to his child. A healthy baby boy named Robert Jr. Since becoming a Dad, Knee began to consider copping out. According to Knee, he had to get home to teach his son the rules of the game. He didn't want his son to grow up to be a punk, rat, or a square and if left up to the child's mother; Robert Jr. would become all of the above. Copping out became for Knee a selfless sacrifice done for a greater good. Robert Jr. was born weighing 5 pounds 5 ounces. J.B. and I silently thanked God for the small miracle.

C-74 housed all adolescents aged sixteen to twenty-one. There were however a handful of adult housing units in the building as well. We called the adults *coffee drinkers* because no true adolescent would be caught dead drinking that mud. Though our living quarters were separated, we shared everything else with the adults. One day while marching down the long corridor that connects the housing units to the mess hall, we spotted coffee drinkers coming our way. I'd been itching for some action; looking for something to get into when I spotted, from a distance, one of the adults wearing a nice piece of shine on his neck. Without a second thought I told Sha to hold me down.

"What up Kay. Talk to me."

Sha was clueless to my intentions and I had no time to put him on point without giving myself away. As our two lines began to walk past each other, our natural reaction was to let it be known who we be and so we began chanting...

"4 Main, house of pain. House of pain, 4 Main!"

The adults smirked as they walked by, clearly reminiscing on their adolescent days. As the dude with the chain approached, I leapt catching him off guard. I was able to yap the chain off his neck with one hand and lick my razor across his face with the other. Quickly, I faded back into the bosom of my line before his reaction really kicked in. Initially, all the adults were stunned at my move and it didn't take long for fists to start flying. Pure pandemonium broke loose. I threw the chain in my mouth and commenced to cutting me some coffee drinkers.

If I hadn't witnessed it with my own eyes, I would never have believed it. The old timers, witnessing their own blood being shed, disengaged from combat and fled. They literally ran! We were still hyped by the time the riot squad arrived and it would have taken nothing for us to set it off again. They saw our readiness and decided against a physical confrontation. Instead we were escorted back to our cells and ordered to lock in. 4 Main was locked down for three days pending an investigation. Our first day off lock down, we marched into the mess hall chanting our chant. I wore the chain for all to see. There were two adult houses already seated and eating, while other adolescents were on the chow line being served.

The adults were paying us no mind, as if they didn't even know we existed. Sha and I still scanned the crowd looking for my nemesis. Neither of us spotted him. As I approached the table to eat, I noticed that those who were in line in front of me were all standing. At first I was confused until I realized what exactly was taking place. They were all waiting for me to sit, and as soon as I did everyone standing followed suit. I noted that even though the adults paid it no mind; the police were clearly paying attention to the impressive display of unity.

As for the adults, they knew better than to step out of line. They saw the force and realized the outcome. They were nothing but a bunch of puss-**BLAM!!** A cup of Kool-Aid sailed silently through the air until blasting one of the home team square in the head. Before we knew it we were being bombarded with trays, cups, and fruits from all angles. The coffee drinkers weren't lamed out after all. They rocked us to sleep, leading us to believe it was over. They didn't let up. They came at us swinging trays and other make shift weapons.

My adrenaline was flowing. This was my element. It was like one big game to me. Instinctively, both Sha and I spit out our razors and went to work. To this day I don't know if it was a cup or a piece of fruit, but what ever it was struck me hard. I remember getting up off the floor disoriented and vulnerable. While on the floor I must've dropped my razor because I no longer was in possession of it. I knew that it was lost in the melee of the event. Standing there watching the spectacle unfold around me, feeling a little dizzy, I didn't see my bandit creeping up on me from behind. Not until the last minute when the ice pick was about to plunge into my kidney. I spun away from his swing, but he still tore flesh.

All I could do was dance, bluff and stall, pretending as if I still had the razor in my hand. I faked a few swings. My bandit was reluctant to really rock. He had been cut by me already and clearly was afraid of being cut again. His caution saved me. A mop ringer descended upon his head with resounding force. I heard the crack of his skull. It was simultaneous with the gas cans exploding. Rapidly the place filled with gas while all around me a harsh melody of coughing and choking became law. Everyone was covering their mouths and nostrils with their shirts. Through the fog I saw my man Ice, one of the dudes who robbed Raquel Welch drop the mop ringer and cover his face. I knew I owed him one for coming to my rescue. Again I escaped another close call.

I was identified as the ringleader and placed in 1-Lower bing. I was given sixty-five days in the bing (solitary confinement), which was a lot back then. It was my first time being placed in solitary confinement and boy I literally thought the fuckin' walls were closing in on me. After the second week, however, things began to change. I began enjoying the time alone. Never before had I spent so much time in deep thought.

I thought about my childhood, those years before the robberies, when it was just me and J.B. We would go fishing for tadpoles in Prospect Park, returning home with muddy shoes and pant legs. All day long we would practice our *bunny hops* and *pop wheelies* on our dirt bikes.

I thought about our dear mother; how hard she tried to keep us on the straight path. Realizing how painful it must be having both her sons in prison, I thought of how helpless she must've felt. I remember writing her a long letter telling her that she wasn't a failure; that she hadn't let us down. I thought about Alicia and admitted for the first time to myself that I was in love.

When my thoughts would turn dark, I always ended up thinking about Precious, Smooth and Smiley; the demonic trinity. I began creating different scenarios of revenge. Using the entire cell as my theater, I would literally play out the different scenes of vengeance I created. It was in the bing that I learned of Precious' pregnancy by Smooth. From all accounts she was the first lady of Bed-Stuy. It was the type of fuel I needed to keep the hate alive.

Meanwhile, all hell broke loose in population. The adolescents against the adults melee had spun completely out of control. An adult named *Harry-O* stabbed *Little Herc* from Queens in the neck and paralyzed him. Practically everyday afterwards riot alarms kept all inhabitants of the building awake. It was open field's day on the adults. Even cool ass J.B. found himself caught up in the drama and in an ironic twist of fate wound up directly across from me in the bing for fifteen days.

The closer I got to getting out of the bing the more restless I grew. Anticipation of my return to the war front kept me awake and from all the reports I received, the troops were waiting for my morale boost as well.

Sha came to the bing about a month later for knocking out *Captain Kliene*. The racist captain had been asking for an ass whuppin' for years. Everyone knew that he sported a tattoo on his shoulder depicting a Black baby with a rope around its neck hanging from a tree. The riot squad whupped Sha's ass; a beating he graciously accepted, even the cracked ribs and broken jaw.

Knee was back in population and for the first time in his life his focus was on something other than his rep. He began hustling with Jah-Loyal, trying to make some money he could send home to help out with his child. In the war between young and old, Jah-Loyal was trying to play peacemaker, claiming to be neutral. He considered himself a businessman and war was bad for business.

For me, that was the final straw. Not only had Jah provided a sanctuary for Trey, but also when Trey went home Jah plugged him in with his brother Bad. One day during mail call, I received a letter with no return address. A single photo sat inside the envelope. It was a photo of Trey sitting in the driver's seat of a white '87 Maxima counting money. On the back of the photo he wrote...

"While you focus on fame; I'm mastering the game!"
That was Jah's doing. It sounded like something he would say and now he was secretly trying to squash the beef and undermine my bully. I was upset with Knee as well for going along with the coward.

Finally, released from isolation I was placed in 2-Lower. Because it sat in the bowels of the building; we called it *the dungeon*. My man Ice and his co-defendant Jabbar, were running the house; the red carpet was laid out in my honor. Without any inquiry I was given the 8-9:30 p.m. phone slot. Having long ago married his reputation to mine, Ice went out of his way to make me feel comfortable. He understood that the General had landed.

It didn't take long to discover that Ice was a dictator with a dark sense of humor. I began calling him *Bully* due to the tyrannical way he ran the dungeon. Ice had a team of servants always on standby. There were two lackeys whose duties consisted of doing the house's laundry by hand. All day they sat in front of the bathroom's slop sink washing clothes and scrubbing underwear. Their hands being submerged in water for hours at a time, resembled even when dry, withered and discolored prunes. Instead of shame these morons took pride in their job and the fifteen minutes a piece of phone time Ice gave them.

Blimpie, Ice's Christian name for another underling had nothing to do with him being fat. He was given this name by Ice as a term of endearment because of the pride Blimpie took in his job. He was the sandwich man whose duty was to hook up sandwiches for the executive team whenever we got hungry. It was not uncommon for him to be woken out of his sleep and given the order.

"Yo Blimpie...we need twenty turkey and cheeses and go light on the mayo this time."

Besides the domestic help, Ice also employed a team of entertainers. A tall, bamboo thin character Ice named *Sony* took the cake. He was awarded this name because his sole function was to rap and sing for us on demand. For my listening pleasure Bully made Sony sing a bunch of old rap songs for three hours straight. Wherever we went he followed us around singing. Sony's mouth turned frothy white in need of water, but Ice in his dark humor said...

> "*I thought you wanted to be a rapper? You think RUN-DMC stops for water? Man don't stop until I tell you to.*"

Whenever I think back to that day I smile. Because who would've thought then that within less than a decade Sony would become a multi-millionaire rap icon. Yeah, nowadays he goes by a different name, but forgive me for fast-forwarding too far.

The funniest moment of my first day in the dungeon occurred when a new-jack entered the house. Immediately Ice stepped to him, the wolves one step behind. I leaned up against the wall indifferent to what was about to take place. Having witnessed this scenario play out a thousand times with the only difference being the faces of the actors involved in the drama.

"*Yo shorty...where you from.*"
"*My name ain't shorty!*"
"*Word? What's your name then?*"
"*D-D-Dereck.*"
"*That's cool shorty...but where you from?*"

Shorty looked around nervously realizing that fifty pairs of eyes were staring coldly at him. Comprehending finally, that he was in the proverbial hot seat and the quality of his answers would determine his fate.

"*Harlem.*"
"*Word shorty? Where at in Harlem?*"
"*148th and Amsterdam.*"
"*Sugar Hill?*"
"*Yeah...you from Harlem?*"

Shorty asked, a ray of hope emanated from his question.

"*Look shorty...I do the interrogating here-ya follow?*"

Shorty looked at Ice briefly with a mask of defiance. *This might get interesting. I thought.*

"*You know Woody with the red hair?*"
"*Woody... Woody...*"

Shorty was trying to place a face to the name. Ice continued...

"*Yeah man...he laughs funny.*"

Ice was talking about none other than *Wood Woodpecker* but shorty didn't catch on.

"Oh! Woody... I know who you're talking about now, he hangs out with Ron Black and them down on 143rd."

With that fictitious response the death warrant was signed. Ice smiled.

"Yeah...that's him. What about Bugsy with the big teeth?"

"Bugsy?"

"Yeah...sometimes they call him Bugs. He wears gray a lot."

"Nah...I don't know him."

"You mean to tell me you're from Sugar Hill but don't know Bugs? What about little Rocky?"

"Rocky...yeah I know Rocky. He's from Polo Grounds right? Got a sister named Dee Dee."

"Oh...I don't know his sister. How she look? She got a fatty or what?"

"Who...Dee Dee? Nah...she's a crack head. Maybe back in the days she looked good but now..."

Ice interrupted,

"Like I said shorty...I don't know his sister but I know he runs with this tall muthafucka who looks like a moose. His name is Bo something."

"Oh...I know who you're talking about but I forgot his name."

"What's up with them dudes? They chillin' or what?"

"Yeah. Yo Rocky's my man. We go to Skate Key all the time together."

Immediately Ice's expression turned cold.

"Man...those punks tried to rob me."

Shorty clearly was clueless on how to respond. Ice on the other hand was obviously just warming up.

"What about Pete?"

"Pete? Is that the only name he goes by?"

"Well...I think his last name is Parker or something like that?"

Slowly Shorty caught on.

"That's Spider Man!"
A burst of laughter erupted from the crowd. Shorty began laughing with them as if the joke wasn't on him.

It took less than a second for the razor in Ice's mouth to fly into his hand; its sharp edge pressing comfortably against shorty's cheek while his other hand held shorty's head firmly in place. All humor in Ice's eyes was gone replaced by a fire of single-minded determination. Ice's voice descended into a grave whisper.

"Yo Shorty...take those kicks and pants off-now."

He was referring to the brand new pair of Fila and the black acid wash Guess jeans Shorty wore. Paralysis was quickly gripping Shorty - the full court press was on. The crowd stood in silent anticipation. If there was any buck at all left in Dereck the time to reveal it was now. His window of opportunity to escape eternal peonage was just about shut. Nervously he looked around searching for an ally. He found none. It was now or never. I finally understood what swallowing your pride meant. Swallowing hard pleading his case, all to no avail.

"What am I gonna wear?"
Ice quickly barked an order to one of his soldiers.

"Yo...go bring me a pair of Bozo's and those pin stripe Lee's."

Like so many others before him, Shorty failed the pressure test. Call it what you want but these types of trials were a necessary evil amongst adolescents at war. In here there was no such thing as a victim. We were all predators. It wasn't college, it was jail, where the predator in you was tested in a jungle full of carnivores. Unfortunately for Shorty he was now relegated to the bottom of the wild life food chain. I saw enough. While Ice was content with destroying herbs I was already waist deep in my plot to once again shake the building to its core.

Most of the official adults, the ones with heart, were transferred days before I was released. They went to the other adult buildings. The coffee drinkers that were left wanted no part in the onslaught that was about to befall them. There was no honor in pushing punks around and so I accepted the truce.

Besides, no true general will willingly fight on two battlefronts. Another war was on my mind; fertile territory that needed to be conquered.

Before the building could enjoy any calm, I snatched Jah's chain and tried to cut him as he came off the visiting floor. It was easier than I thought it would be. Jah had been in the building for ten months without really being battle tested. His money insulated him. He thought he was untouchable.

I called him. He stopped. We were in the corridor right behind the visiting floor. He had two of his soldiers with him; they looked bored. Like I said they were really comfortable.

"*A yo...good looking on that move you made.*"
He smiled and asked me what move. Like lightening I struck ripping four chains off his neck.
"*That's for Trey faggot!*"

I began walking away, my soldiers covering my retreat. Jah began following me still speechless. I jumped at him and swung hard trying to rip his fuckin' face off-I missed. My attempt stopped him dead in his tracks. I began to walk off again.

"*YOU DONE STARTED SOME SHIT YOU AIN'T READY FOR* ", he yelled.
I looked back and smiled. Little did he know I was born ready.

*   *   *

A HALFWAY CROOK IS A CROOK WITH A CONFLICTED CONSCIENCE WHO GAVE INTO A CONNIVING WHISPER DEPLORING HIM TO TURN HIMSELF IN, OR MAKE A CONFESSION, OR WORSE...RETURN THE SPOILS. THAT WHISPER IS NOT FROM ALLAH, JESUS, OR GOD. IT'S THE WHISPER OF INSANITY FASTLY APPROACHING. BEWARE – BLOCK IT OUT. CALM YOUR MIND.
EXCERPT FROM THE O.G. BIBLE

*   *   *

J.B. and Knee were furious. Though their reasons differed their conclusions were the same. J.B. felt I was prop hunting, trying to keep my name ringing. Knee's position was that my actions threatened the business he was conducting with Jah. For me it was personal. Jah stuck his nose in my business-twice. Never before had I openly gone against J.B. and Knee. We were a team; three the hard way. So I listened to their concerns and plans to avoid what to me was unavoidable. For my part, I agreed not to attack. That was as much as I was willing to concede. J.B. and Knee were supposed to meet with Jah to try to negotiate a peace. I was hoping Jah was full of pride, consumed with revenge and thirsty for blood like I was. You could imagine how disappointed I was when J.B. told me a meeting was set up for me to speak with Jah in the Law Library Friday night.

"*What's there to talk about? Ain't shit to talk about, fuck that bird!*" I was venting.

"*Word to mutha, I'm not with all that SAP rappin' shit. The first slick shit that comes out his mouth I'm letting loose.*"

J.B. had heard enough.

"*You are going to meet with the dude and try to avoid unnecessary drama. Our focus should be entirely on our cases; on getting home as soon as possible. I don't know about you but this caged in shit is for the birds! It's like you enjoy this shit! This ain't no Fresh Air Fund! This is jail!*"

I began to respond but I saw my big brother's eyes watering up. Tears that had nothing to do with a jail house beef. My brother was afraid; scared of getting lost in a merciless system. Afraid of being what he called buried alive.

"*I'll meet him but I'm not giving the chains back.*"

His look silenced any further comment; or perhaps it was my childish response. For amongst brothers some things need never be uttered.

Friday, I walked into the crowded Law Library, razor in my mouth and a fiberglass pick on my waist. I saw all the familiar and expected faces. All the live wires were there; some openly declaring their allegiance to a side; others keeping their cards close to their breast. *If shit pops off tonight, at least we'll see where everyone stands.* I spotted Jah. He was seated in the back. I greeted my Comrades, and grilled my adversaries as I leisurely made my way toward Jah.

"*What's poppin'?*"

"*Have a seat.*"

I looked around one more time and sat directly across from him with only a table and air between us. My neck was flooded with chains including the four I took from him. If that didn't provoke him nothing else would. Yet, he paid the jewelry no mind and got right down to business.

> "*Check it...I spoke with your brothers and I agree with them. If we go to war it's gonna split the building, and a divided building is bad for business.*"

I wasn't there to SAP rap and so I just listened.

> "*I'm in jail for not controlling my emotions. For letting a clown pull the beast out of me.*"

Was he indirectly calling me a *clown*?

> "*I'm supposed to be swimming in some pussy right now, instead of sitting across from a little dude who robbed me.*"

*Little dude...*my eyes lit up. Perhaps we were going to get it on after all. J.B. came to mind and I decided to let that '*little dude*' crap slide-just once. He continued...

> "*I dig your heart, but you are wasting that courage on trinkets.*" Oh boy...here comes the lecture.

> "*I'm not here to try to lecture you, but like I told J.B.-in exchange for letting you keep my shit...*"

I interrupted, "*Fuck all this SAP rap. We could rock and roll right now.*"

I was tight. *Little dude...let me keep the chains...*this clown hit a nerve. But again avoiding the bait, he remained calm and continued...

"All your major beefs stem from you taking trinkets. You robbed Smooth and got shot up."

He was really pushing his luck.

"You robbed the old timer and started some big shit. Your boy Sha got broke up and put in the bing for six months behind the drama and Little Herc might not ever walk again...all for trinkets."

The way he said it made me feel petty.

"Now, let's say we do go to war over four punk ass chains."

Like a slave accused of flirting with a white woman, he let the question hang. As tight as I was I knew he was right. The casualties far outweighed the value of the trinkets. Like J.B. said, I was prop hunting at the expense of my Comrades. My Mother called me selfish. Was this what she meant? I felt uncomfortable. I had the four chains on my neck. It was my victory and yet I felt like the loser, the victim of my own stupidity. I looked at Jah and realized without even lifting a finger he won the war. I guess that's why he was considered the God Father.

Jah agreed to dead the beef. I made no attempt to give back the chains and he never attempted to coerce me to do so. When we shook hands, we looked each other square in the eyes. Both of us searching for a deceptive sign; finding none, we turned to the crowd. There were smiling faces looking back at us. But I knew that many of the smiles only masked the disappointment that was in their hearts. War had been avoided-something only true gladiators could appreciate. Most of these smiling faces were mercenaries and I suspected that once again I would have lost to the highest bidder.

After that day, Jah and I began to kick it. I mean really kick it. He began explaining the nuances of the drug game to me. From measurements to quality I learned it all. He taught me how to cut dope and cook crack. Jah was a good teacher and as time proved, I was an excellent student. More than all those basic instructions, Jah taught me how to organize a team and the psychology behind the hustle. I thought dudes had been exaggerating when they claimed Jah was sending thousands

HONOR AMONGST THIEVES

home weekly; until I witnessed it with my own eyes. He put five grand in my hand to count. I knew it was a test to see if I would pull a stunt. I'm not gonna lie...the thought definitely crossed my mind, but I finally caught a glimpse of the bigger picture and was committed to living it.

For starters, Jah began selling me half ounces of coke for $300. Selling blow proved lucrative. I was able to clear $1600 off a ½ an ounce in a week. I went to Jah ready to buy an ounce but he explained to me that it was wiser to have cash than a lot of product and so I stuck with my ½ ounce. It also became abundantly clear that the coffee drinkers were my biggest clientele and the absence of war did-spell money. It was basic logic to tell you the truth. In a prison environment, who had time to enjoy their high when they were constantly looking over their shoulders? I began to appreciate Jah's insight.

Stacking those chips was my focus for the next few months, when J.B. finally negotiated a plea deal for us. Because, Knee was already on five years probation for robbery at the time of our arrest his cop-out was the highest. He pled to a 7-21yrs, while J.B. took a 6-18yrs. Because I was a minor at the time of our arrest, I was given a 1 ½ - 4 ½. However, my case for the bulletproof vest was still pending and for me, more time was promised.

J.B. and Knee were relieved; they both had seventeen months in on the cases already. They were ready to go *up north* and once again we were about to be separated. That same month, however, was the month of final outcomes for many.

Big Sha copped out to 8 1/3-25yrs for murder 2°. Money Mike copped out to a 3-9, while Baby Grand blew trial and was sentenced to 18 to life. His co-defendant, James Young, aka *Knowledge* became the star witness against him. Jah got a mistrial and was very optimistic about going home. The very next day after our sentencing, Knee was sent upstate. Usually, a person was given about a month before being sent up but they wanted Knee out of the building in the worst way.

I still remember the day we were all hanging out in the deserted yard standing on the frozen bleachers. Even for the month of February, it was cold. The previous day I copped out to a year running wild for the bulletproof vest. This meant that instead of a 1 ½ - 4 ½, I now had 2 ½ - 4 ½. J.B. had gone upstate two weeks before and I was expected to leave any day. My stay on Rikers Island was coming to an end and so we were in the yard celebrating my pending departure, talking that gangsta talk and passing the blunts around. It was me, Jah, Kevin McDuffy, Puerto Roc, Touchy, Dominican June and Stan standing in a circle passing the blunts around when *Red Hook Rod* brought the news. Smooth and Smiley were found murdered in an apartment in Queens.

    I didn't believe it. I refused to believe it. My high was blown-someone stole my thunder. As night descended, the truth of the *grisly murders* was discussed on every news channel in N.Y. No leads, no witnesses, and in the streets people were already whispering…speculating. Smooth was going to war with a gorilla out of Bushwick named *Pop*. He was the dude Smooth thought sent me to rob him. No one really believed Pop had the patience or cunning to get that close to Smooth. Thus, it didn't take long for my name to start making the circuit and before you knew it, as far as the hood was concerned-I was responsible.

    What made this theory convincing was they were murdered within hours of my sentencing. Jah jokingly inquired as to what I'd been doing with all the money I was making. But his eyes betrayed him and I knew he wasn't joking. He suspected me of finally becoming the highest bidder. *Not yet. Not yet.* I know now, all these years later, what exactly happened to Smooth but at the time I was clueless. The only question that kept invading my thoughts-where was Precious? I had a nagging feeling that I was the only one thinking about her-just the way she wanted it. As expected the homicide detects came to see me. I refused to answer any questions and kept asking to call my lawyer. Eventually they left. The next morning I found myself on a bus heading upstate; heading in fact-to a new world.

    *   *   *

CHAPTER 9
AT THE FEET OF THE MASTER

The first four prisons I went to rejected me. *Coxsackie*, a maximum prison for adolescents never allowed me out of its receiving room. Somehow, a written threat on my life mysteriously appeared and I was on my way to *Comstock*. Yet, once again, with a little added spice, I was denied entry there as well. Another threat on my life materialized. Initially I was flattered. Being rejected from a prison seemed gangsta. But when *Clinton* rejected me; then while attending orientation in *Elmira* my cell was set on fire, did the seriousness of the danger I was in begin to scare me.

J.B. was in *Greenhaven*, while both Knee and Sha were in *Comstock*. So wherever I was headed, I was on my own. In Elmira, I was placed in Involuntary Protective Custody, or *IPC* while they attempted to figure out what to do with me. IPC was similar to being in the box, with the exception being instead of a twenty-three hour lockdown I was locked down twenty hours a day. It was while in IPC that a dude explained to me exactly what was happening. All along I was under the impression, that a bunch of cowards didn't want me making it into population. That couldn't have been further from the truth. They weren't trying to keep me out, they were sending, or flushing me into the trap they wanted. I was being flushed to a prison where my death would be a certainty. Insomnia kicked in. Sleep became impossible-I was afraid. J.B., Knee and Sha wrote, warning me of what must be in the mix. As thorough as they were, they were powerless to stop it. Up north their reps held no weight. Sure they would avenge it, but stop it?

I thought of all my enemies and only Smooth-the corpse could possibly command such support. Compared to him all else were small fries. What made shit even worse was my enemies were faceless, and the prison where the trap was to be sprung...still a mystery. After the latest incident, the administration realized what was taking place. They offered me a protective custody spot disguised as an honor job. They called it *cadre*.

Immediately, I refused. Despite the fear, my pride and courage would not let me die a thousand deaths-if it was to be-then it would be warrior style and nothing less. For two months I lingered in *Elmira's* IPC until I was finally moved to *Auburn* Correctional Facility. Was this the trap? Would *Auburn* be the arena or just another pit stop?

When I made it through two days of reception without being flushed, I had my answer. *Auburn* was where it was going to pop off. An entire week in reception went by without a hitch, and I was finally placed in population. Despite the anxiety I was feeling the freedom of movement felt good. When the officer came by my cell and asked me if I wanted to go to *rec*, without a second thought I said…

"*Yeah…*"

I had two gem stars, and truly believed I was armed and loaded.

When I reached the rec yard a familiar face quickly emerged. It was my man *Damien* from the South Side who greeted me. I knew Dame well enough to know he wasn't part of any plot. I also didn't want to drag him into something not meant for him. After five minutes of catching up on past adventures I told him I would check him in a few minutes. I began stepping, surveying the mine field, looking for the glitches and finding none. This disturbed me; whoever was behind this was playing it correctly. No signs of attack were present. Finally I pulled up against a wall and waited. For three hours nothing happened. Then the call…

"*Rec is now over!*"

…came and my opponent still had not materialized.

The following morning I awoke to a face of my past. It had been at least seven years since I saw it. I was playing skelly when the police took it away. The face belonged to *Swift*, one of Knee's brothers. He was grinning in the very same way Knee does when he has pulled one over on you.

"*Little Kay Kay…what's the deal?*"
"*Hey Swift! WHAT UP?*"

> *"Man you tell me! Your name's been ringin' bells for a good minute now. I hear you've been climbin' up the food chain pretty quickly."*

I smiled at the compliment and returned the gesture.

> *"Well I learned from the best ya know."*

Of course I was talking about Knee, but Swift wasn't swift enough to catch it. His grin became a smile from ear to ear.

> *"Check it. Come to the yard this afternoon. There's someone I want you to meet."*

Could Swift be a part of the conspiracy? Would he betray Knee? As if reading my suspicions Swift continued...

> *"I got a kite from Knee about two weeks ago explaining what was taking place. Personally I ain't got enough pull to intercept a flush on the scale that it's coming. You stopped some serious gorillas from eating-but I did know of one old timer with the strength to intercept it. On the strength that you're my little brother's, little homey, I spoke up for you."*

I guess I should have been relieved but all that kept going through my mind was this *little shit* he kept babbling. Instead of thanking him I asked him;

> *"Who dis kat I'm supposed to meet?"*

> *"He's an old timer. You'll see when you get there. Anyway, here take this..."*

He began to pass me cosmetics, shower slippers and a load of junk food through the bars.

> *"Yo...I'll see you in the yard little homey."*

And with that he was gone. *Why had Swift been so evasive in his answer?* Out of six brothers, Swift was the second to last, older than Knee by four years and thus my senior by nine. He was in his sixth year of a 7 to life sentence for extortion and gun running charges. A hood icon, given the name Swift because of his legendary knuckle game, but could I trust him? I knew I had no choice. Even thugs must sometimes bungee jump on faith, besides he was Knee's brother. Since Knee trusted him, so would I. Anything else would have been uncivilized.

When I hit the yard, I sensed that the atmosphere shifted from the day before. I could also tell from the lingering glares that my presence was no longer anonymous; that the word was obviously out-Kameek Barnes has landed.

"*Fuck it. Let's get this shit over with.*"

I started walking through the yard until I spotted Swift standing up against the wall with a handful of dudes. They saw me approaching and just stared. Swift gave me a pound, turned to the dudes he was with and told them he would be back. As we walked away I could feel their stares penetrating my back like an x-ray. It didn't bother me; my head was held high-a clear indication that my backbone wasn't missing.

Swift escorted me past the weights and bleachers to the back of the yard; the furthest possible point away from the nearest C.O. Two old timers were talking, Swift spoke to one. He was tall, high yellow and bald, wearing a thick pair of Gazelle glasses. I figured him to be about sixty. As Swift spoke to him, the old timer shook his head affirmatively as if whatever Swift was saying all made sense. Finally the old timer looked at me, said a few words to the scarecrow he had been in conversation with, then approached me. A firm hand was extended my way.

"*I'm the Old God. Pleased to meet you.*"

THE OLD GOD!!! That legendary name right up there with Carlos the Jackal? Could this man standing before me really be the character of legend? An ex Black Panther who used armed struggle to keep the corrupt cops out of Bed-Stuy. The man the dope dealers betrayed and set up to be executed. Legend has it, that when the Old God learned of the covert contract between the police and the hustlers he brought the wrath to both.

When the smoke cleared four hustlers and three police were dead, two others were badly wounded while the Old God lay bleeding with five gun shot wounds to the chest and head. This happened in '68, a few months after the death penalty had been rescinded in N.Y. The Old God escaped the chair but not life in prison.

If the Black Panthers were a national image of black manhood-the Old God was the warrior image for N.Y. He spent my entire existence behind bars and yet his name was still being spoken of in the smoked filled rooms and hallways of the concrete jungle. I extended my hand - and greeted him the way a Five Star General was meant to be greeted - with sincerity.

For the next two hours we spoke about my struggle or what the Old God termed my *causes and effects*. He didn't say much, only interrupting at times for clarification. I found myself sharing thoughts with him that I kept guarded and close to my heart. His debriefing was thorough. I felt as if a load had been lifted off my shoulders. It wasn't until the last hour of our conversation that I learned the particulars of the flush.

Smooth did a three year bid from '78 to '81. In that time he made a few alliances with a number of individuals who would never see the streets again. When Smooth began making money he made sure that those left behind benefited from his success as well. Practically every maximum facility in the state of N.Y. was being supplied heroin and coke by Smooth via his allies. Needless to say his death put a serious dent in the prison's economy.

Never once did the Old God ask me whether or not I had anything to do with Smooth's death. For him, it would've been a rhetorical question: 1) he wouldn't have expected me to answer honestly and 2) as I would learn in the following months - Smooth's death was irrelevant to the Old God's view. Nevertheless, it was in Attica where the flush was supposed to send me-where my death was to be a certainty. The Old God then laid the cards on the table.

"I don't deal with knuckle heads and anyone who deals with me plays by these rules; it's all about respect. Give everyone including the hacks respect. You do this because in return you demand nothing less. Speak only when directly spoken to and not before. Otherwise, keep your mouth shut. This is not The Fever or some other nightclub, this is prison. You're not here to mingle and become popular. You're here to survive."

The Old God looked to see if I comprehended all he just stated. I nodded my head in affirmation and he continued...

"Avoid making or reacting to indirect statements. Cowards speak in sweeping terms-men address issues

directly and without an audience. If you have any hidden hopes of becoming an NBA or NFL player when you get out and you are planning to work on your skills while you are in here - kill that notion. Men deal in reality - kids play games and deal in dreams. Sports in prison breeds familiarity. Familiarity breeds disrespect. Lastly, pay close attention to everything but remember to see nothing, understood?"

I nodded. It was my first humbling experience but when it came to the Old God it wouldn't be my last. Before we left the yard I asked the Old God why he intervened on my behalf.

"I didn't intervene, I intercepted...there's a difference. Your life is still on the market. I just made the reward more perilous to collect. But that doesn't mean for one moment that even here, under my domain, an attempt to get at you won't be made.
Do you have arms besides the two razors in your mouth?"

"Nah."

"Well then...the first order of business is to get you some bigger muscles."

And with that my tutelage began.

To intervene is to negotiate, to reconcile, while to intercept means to seize or stop its course. As the Old God would drill in me over and over, *words are key - they have power.* I learned how to be very analytical of the words used by others and the words I chose to use. For in analyzing words, I was able to really understand what a person was and wasn't saying.

Prison was a great deal more complicated for me to adjust to than jail. In jail the routine, rules and protocol were easy to learn. In fact, even easier to change. Prison, however is a place of unsaid rules firmly entrenched like the bobbed wire that gives it its structure. Ever present and menacing, some rules are revealed only after living and experiencing the mistakes of not knowing them. I heard a lot about prison, mostly war stories, yet nothing prepared me for the overwhelming loneliness and hopelessness that lingers in prison air. J.B.'s term of being buried alive, bore flesh before my very eyes.

Nighttime in prison is full of guarantees, such at the muffled sounds of crying men locked in their cells, staring at photos and facsimiles of loved ones and good times lost forever. What does one say to someone whose continued existence, promises not a ray hope; and yet everyday for decades they've managed to find a meaning. Here, the law of the jungle is set by the vision of these men and no one, especially a skid bidder like me, would ever change the flow.

In the daytime I was in school pursuing my GED and in the evening I walked the yard or hit the weights with the Old God. Despite popular belief there are no state of the art-Jack La Lane type-gyms in prison. Auburn Correctional Facility confirmed this truth. The weight area was located in the corner of the main yard. Only twelve weight courts for the entire population's use and so an elaborate schedule was established amongst the prisoners to ensure that everyone had access to the weights.

Two weight courts belonged to the Whites who were clearly the minority. The Spanish Brothers had four courts, which again was befitting their numbers. The remaining six courts were divided amongst the Blacks. But not all Blacks were welcome on these courts. I quickly learned that in prison while all other racial groups displayed a semblance of unity-we were the only ones visibly divided.

The Muslims saw themselves as something beyond Black, a colorless soldier of Allah if you will. They called everyone who wasn't Muslim-*Kafars*, which simply means non-believers. But the way they used this word was similar to a Southern Cracker calling a Black Man-boy.

The Five Percenters were the elitist. They viewed themselves as the enlightened ones whose greatest weapon was their thousand dollar vocabulary. Those of us who weren't Gods were called *Eighty Fivers*-on account that we were deaf, dumb and blind-savages in the pursuit of happiness. Then there was the Caribbean court. Though comprised of a mixture of nationalities from Panamanians to Jamaicans, they were united in their view and opinion of Blacks born in Babylon. According to them the Yankee boys were lazy complainers whose deepest desire was to become a White Man. Because of this rootlessness, the urge to imitate and love the White Man, we *Yankee boys* could not be trusted.

The Christian Brothers were the guys whose conversion to Christ always seemed convenient and calculated; a way to hide. Due to their religious affinity with the officers and administration, they were given extra privileges. While the Muslims, Gods and Yardies all had their share of the pie-the Christians with their link to the administration was the biggest protection agency in the penal.

Then there were the rest of us Blacks. The forsaken. The deaf, dumb and blind Babylonian Kafars-sinners headed towards purgatory. The lost. Diverse in our walks of life-from gangstas to gamblers, gunmen to bank robbers and sons to grandfathers. In the hood, I never saw a congregation of this many grandfatherly types. It was as if Auburn was the cheapest retirement home for aging Black Men. And yet, despite the abundant presence of the old timers, we were still a divided nation. Not due to bloodshed but foreign ideologies and *better than you* attitudes.

I made mention of my observations to the Old God one winter's night. We were on the workout court reserved exclusively for the Old God and his companions of like mind. He shook his head sagely but gave no response. Instead he went back under the weight. We were doing chest on the incline bench and the Old God was about to lift his max of 275 lbs. For a fifty-eight year old man he was extremely strong and well fit. '*Relentless'* was his motto when it came to working out.

Like me, most guys work out strictly for the women but the Old God worked out for the sole purpose of staying fit for war.

"*Youngin' it's not about looking fit, it's about being fit.*"
The Old God heaved the first four reps with professional ease then gritted out the remaining four with a primal push of pure determination. The cold of the night bounced off his head as if being repelled by a force field. He took a deep breath then

exhaled. Like *Puff the Magic Dragon* smoke escaped his lips. He stood up and said...

"*You know youngin', very few people are able to make an observation like that in such a short time. Tell me...do you believe that this is the reason for our disunity?*"

"*Yeah...I guess so.*"

The Old God put his wool hat and gloves on-zipped up his brown quilted parka jacket, said his fair wells to our other workout partners, turned my way and said...

"*Let's walk.*"

To keep our body temperatures warm we walked fast and furious. Around the yard we went, all the time observant of our hostile surroundings. After a couple of silent laps the Old God began to speak; his voice projecting a distance, as if somehow he had been transported back in time.

"*After serving two tours in Korea I came home in the summer of '63. I was told that the Koreans were my enemy but never told why. I fought hard in that war and lost a lot of good friends. But nothing prepared me for the real enemy's attack on my neighborhood. I came back to a neighborhood that was no longer neighborly. I never saw a weapon produce more lethal consequences on an unsuspecting civilian population than heroin. And what amazed me was that it seemed as if I was the only one who saw it for what it truly was. So many of my friends and even my younger brother was nodding and scratching. It was like the land of the lost, a sleepwalker's paradise. I was looking for answers and desperately needed to be around like minds. I found myself attending the Audobon on a weekly basis.*"

"*The Audo-who?*" I asked.

"*The Audobon was a ballroom/auditorium up in Washington Heights. It's where Malcolm held his weekly speeches after he left the Nation of Islam.*"

Unconsciously his voice lowered.

"*It's also where Malcolm-the man, not the spirit was murdered.*"

There appeared a resigned sagging in his shoulders as if even after all these years the truth of his statement was still hard to accept. Already knowing the answer I asked...
"*So you really did know Malcolm?*"
"*Yeah...we became pretty good friends.*"
His voice took on a new buoyancy as he stated that fact.
"*He and Herman gave me my first intellectual spankin'.*"
"*Herman?*"
"*Yeah...Herman Fergueson. Malcolm's Minister of Education and one of the many unsung heroes of our people.*"
"*Never heard of him.*"
"*Yeah...most haven't.*"
"*What happened to him?*"
"*Shortly after Malcolm's death, he went into exile-somewhere in Latin America. Cointelpro made him a target and so he found it prudent to expatriate himself.*"
"*Cointelpro?*"
"*Yeah...J. Edgar Hoover's Counter Intelligence Program. It was an FBI operation designed in their own words, 'to stop the rise of a Black Messiah'.*"
It was too much for me to understand so I became an ear.
"*Anyhow, it was Malcolm who first opened my eyes to the Pan African Movement.*"
"*Pan African?*"
"*Yeah...it means all Black People united no matter your religious or intellectual ideology. No matter your tribe, borough or hood-it's all about unity. The media loves to make a big deal about Malcolm's letter referring to his White Muslim Brothers, as if that one paragraph somehow erased all that he stood for and ultimately died for.*"
"*I don't understand, I mean I'm trying to keep up but you're losing me.*" I admitted.
"*Malcolm died because he began focusing on the bigger picture. Because a unified people are a victorious people, Malcolm's move towards Pan Africanism sealed his fate. His organization the O.A.A.U. (Organization

for African American Unity) was going to become that unifying vehicle."

"So when Malcolm died why didn't anyone step up?" I asked.

"That's a very good question youngin'. As a people it seems we tend to follow the Messenger and not the Message. We get so caught up in the charisma and not the plan. So when the enemy kills the leader he kills the plan."

"Why didn't you or Herman step up?"

"Well...Herman was the next target to be neutralized, and as for me, I had the passion but I was still green. I had no idea what running an organization entailed. And besides I wasn't thinking straight. My hero had just been murdered and all I had was ice in my veins and blood in my eyes."

"So what happened to the organization?"

"Ella eventually took it over."

"Ella?"

"Yeah...his older sister."

"So what? She wasn't qualified to hold it down?"

The Old God chuckled at that notion.

"Ella was more than qualified. Black Men just weren't prepared to follow the lead of a Black Woman! It's a psychological sickness; one we inherited from slavery. As for me, I began working with the gangs. I felt they were our sleeping giants. But it was frustrating trying to awaken a beast that wanted to remain asleep. I heard about a group of warriors out in Oakland who were stepping to their business."

"The Panthers", I interrupted.

"Yeah...the Panthers. I went out to Oakland and actually met Huey and Eldridge. They both were younger than me and in many ways a great deal greener. But they had one thing right, one thing that trumped everything else. They understood the need for an armed struggle. They knew we needed an unseen army. And so I joined. I was given the task of establishing a

clandestine army in N.Y.C. You see youngin'...diplomacy becomes nothing more than begging without the threat of force."

Needless to say my thoughts were in a whirlwind at this point. I knew enough to know what the Old God was sharing with me was some next level gangsta shit. Going up against the government was as crazy as it could get. To even think too long on such a subject took a lot of heart. I wanted to ask more but I could see that the Old God was wrestling with the ghost of a painful memory. Beginning to think that my lesson was at an end I glanced at him and was surprised to see that he was measuring his words.

"*I underestimated the power of heroin and the diseased minds it left in its wake. You may have heard that friends betrayed me. The truth is, like Denmark Vessey, I revealed my plans to a diseased mind. It was my fault; I've been in war. I know the rules. Understanding the terrain is the most crucial part of any battle. I failed in my assignment.*"

It was my first history lesson by the Old God and though it wouldn't be my last it was the most profound. For the breaking of a shell reveals a larger world to its occupant, my shell had been shattered and my first glimpse was at destiny.

Perhaps the air upstate really is fresher than the city air because almost immediately I began growing. I grew four inches in eight months and stood at six feet by my seventeenth birthday. I also put on muscle mass, and when I looked in the mirror, I could clearly see the peach fuzz darkening my upper lip. Alicia and my Moms claimed my voice was getting deeper but I couldn't tell the difference.

Twice a month Alicia made the six hour trip to see me and it was on one of those prison visits that I convinced her to pursue her dream of becoming a doctor. Alicia was by far the smartest person I knew. If anyone had the mind for medicine it was her. Every visit she would bring me a new book and quiz me about the previous one. Just as much as I pushed her, Alicia pushed me twice as hard.

> "I'm telling you Kameek the world stands still for no one. Baby, if you don't challenge your mind you're gonna come home useless."

Alicia's piercing green eyes ensnared me. Working her hypnotic voodoo, her quiz would always begin the same way;

> "So tell me what you think about the book"

"It was ayat,"

I always tried my hardest to make her interrogation as difficult as possible. Unfazed Alicia would press on.

> "You did read the book didn't you?"
> "Of course I read the book."
> "Okay, so what did you think?"
> "I thought about you the whole time."

My hand brushing gently across her cheek.

> "Seriously baby, what did you think?"
> "Well, the author spoke about being able to identify the differences between a male, boy and man."
> "Which one would you say you are?"

Alicia asked in all seriousness. I started to crack a joke, but at the last minute I caught myself realizing that only a boy would respond to a serious question with a joke.

> "I'm a man!"

I exclaimed, Alicia looked unconvinced, but was wise enough not to challenge my declaration; instead she followed up with.

> "So what didn't you like about the book?"

Thus the process would continue on this way until she was convinced that I thoroughly read the material. I looked forward to her challenges because it forced me to think beyond the streets.

J.B. was in Greenhaven Correctional Facility, attending college for Sociology. He also became part of an Afro-Centric think tank. Constantly he wrote about the Black Man's struggles and our need to commit ourselves to it. 'I'm telling you Kay…we've been duped all along-read <u>Conspiracy to Destroy Black Boys</u> and tell me what you think.'

Knee was in the box in Comstock for smacking his baby's Moms on the visit. As a result he lost all contact with his

son and every letter he wrote me was filled with ways he was gonna make *the bitch pay...*
> *"As God is my witness, the bitch is doomed. I'm gonna make her ass suffer before I twist her cap."*

Big Sha also enrolled in college taking Liberal Arts...
> *"Main man...my English Professor is a dime piece. She's the only Black Teacher in the whole school building. Dudes be sweating her-but you know she likes her men big-so I'm the top choice hands down (Ha-ha!)."*

I also received confirmation on a bit of information regarding conniving assed Precious. Apparently within days after Smooth and Smiley's murders, Precious and her family vanished. One of her neighbors claimed a light skinned man driving a U-Haul truck came in the middle of the night and moved them and their belongings. Immediately the hood began to suspect either Precious had a hand in the murders or she knew who did. Either way she was gone and if smart, she would never look back. But I couldn't help feeling in my gut our paths were meant to cross again. At least it was my hope.

    As for Jah-Loyal, the unbelievable occurred. His lawyer beat the murder charge for him, but before he could cop out to the drug charge a federal indictment swept him away. Jah's brother and the entire Purple City Posse went down hard. The irony of their predicament...Trey was responsible for their fall.

    Apparently he sold a couple of kilos to an undercover federal agent over the course of a three month period. When they finally snatched him he immediately agreed to *cooperate* and for the next eight months, Trey wore a wire. I thought of Jah and wondered what he must be going through. He taught me a valuable and unforgettable lesson: it truly is possible to outsmart anyone including yourself.

    *   *   *

CHAPTER 10
PEACOCK

My time upstate was empty of real drama. The Old God, in many ways taught me many things. If I had one jewel to pick out of all the rest, I would say it was teaching me how to be decisive in all that I do. Most people fail to execute a successful plan because they entered the operation with too many doubts and fears. According to the Old God, there is no such thing as a *benefit of doubt*. It's either you do or you don't; either you get away or you get caught. It's that simple. There's no reward in second guessing an action, because once the act is committed, the only logical course is to follow through. It is what it is and can never be anything else.

After accepting this jewel, things like getting my GED became simple. I decided to get it and before I knew it I had it. I turned my mind into a magnet and began attracting all my heart's desires. It was like a chain that held me back for so long was finally broken. I was ready to fly the coop. I had goals to accomplish, capital to acquire-in abundance. I felt invincible and if it wasn't for the guidance of the Old God, I might have dangled myself over those prison walls with bed sheets tied together. My spirit became restless.

After countless hours of heavy discussions, the Old God seeing that despite his political lessons, I was still focused on the paper chase, once again slid a jewel to me.

"Man you talk about the paper chase, but don't have a clue where to begin."

I knew he was leading me somewhere.

"What you mean by that?"

"I mean just what I said. What WORD clouded your comprehension?"

The Old God was a teacher who didn't repeat himself so my question was nothing more than rhetorical. The Old God continued...

"All you little niggas talk about going home and making it happen. Yet every year one of you return with an

> asshole full of time or I read about ya death in the newspaper."

The Old God grew quiet as he gathered the rest of his thoughts.

> "The problem with the game is that it is really a game to you clowns. It's not taken seriously. It's a 'look-at-me' game. A game for fuckin' peacocks who like to strut their colorful asses around and play rich. Like little girls playing house, never realizing that at the end of the rainbow waits punishment and pain."

I remained silent, not even bothering to dispute his observations. He'd been in prison close to twenty years. What could he know about the paper chase?

> "To master the game you must become a master and respect all its rules. Name one constitutional Amendment."

I couldn't.

> "What are your rights if you get pulled over by the police while driving a car? What's the difference between getting caught with a fully loaded gun and an inoperable one? What's the advantage of testifying before a grand jury on your own behalf? What's the disadvantage? How are search warrants obtained? What makes a wire tap inadmissible? What is a conspiracy charge? Better yet, why are you looking so dumbfounded? Like I said, you just want to be a fuckin' peacock."

I was stuck on *s* for stupid and needed no acting. Not one question could I answer with certainty-not one. How was I to win in a game without knowing any of the rules? To make matters worse the Old God wasn't through...

> "What do you know about the nature of a man, especially around large quantities of money? It's one thing to know a person when ya both broke and hungry? What happens when the belly starts to fill and the hamburger is no longer big enough to share? When the stage is only big enough for one star? Can you detect smokeless fire, son? Can you?"

He had me there.

"Smokeless fire? You're talking in riddles Old God."
"Am I? Read about it in the Koran. It's the nature of the devil."
"I never read the Bible or the Koran."
"Sure you have stupid-you are a walking Koran and Bible. That devil can be detected in others only by studying it in yourself. Smokeless fire is the desire, greed and envy in man. It's that raging fire that can burn inside while a smile and a kind word remain on the surface. If you can't spot it, then you are one peacock about to enter the wrong game."

When I got back to the cell, I found the wheels in my mind turning a mile a minute. I literally felt like my brain was about to explode. This old muthafucka did it again - left my shit scrambled.

I decided to study the game in earnest. I began going to the Law Library. I started with the U.S., then the N.Y. Constitution. I studied the structure of the government, how laws were made and enforced. Then I went into actual charges; reading cases that exploited loopholes from murder to pick pocketing-from embezzlement to conspiracy. To be a master in the paper chase I needed to know the rules and find loopholes. Back in the cell I began reading autobiographies of successful men, psychology and sociology books and I even dabbled in theology. In the nineteen months I was at Auburn I couldn't name more than twenty-five other prisoners. I was so focused on mastering these rules that I didn't have time to mingle.

Another thing the Old God taught me was to become security conscious. We would spin the yard five-six times talking about various topics, then out of now where, he would ask me where someone was located in the yard or what they were wearing. What show was on the television as we passed by or what was the score of the game? How many guard towers were visible, etc. At first I couldn't answer more than one or two of these questions correctly. Eventually, if I got even one of the questions he asked me wrong, I was upset with myself the rest of the night.

My day of departure was quickly approaching. In two weeks time I was to be a free man again. I saw enough misery and despair to know that I would not be brought back to any prison alive. Between the Old God's lectures and J.B.'s letters, I knew that in America we were the outcasts. Where J.B. felt that through education and politics we could eventually change things; the Old God felt that the only language the government spoke was violence. If we don't communicate in that native tongue, we might as well be talking gibberish. I saw it differently. I believed that to change anything, we first had to accumulate wealth and therefore I was committed to the paper chase.

Finally...my last week arrived and I could sense the Old God's withdrawals. The closer I came to leaving the greater distance he gave me. The last time I saw him, we were in the yard kicking it when he left to go to the bathroom. Swift got hit at the parole board the day before and I was listening to his cry for freedom when a fight broke out.

Quickly, shit escalated and before I knew it three dudes were swinging makeshift knives at two other kats reminiscent of a scene straight out of *The Gladiator*. Immediately I looked for the Old God and spotted him walking nonchalantly toward me observing the fight. Suddenly a gun shot broke our hypnosis. It was followed by a command from the guard tower...

"Everyone get the fuck on the ground face first! Hands on your head!"

I was startled and immediately followed everyone else. Then I heard the rattle of another shot and the repeated warning to get the fuck on the ground. I dared to look up. What emotions coursed through my body at that moment to this day I cannot truly say. Was it pride, fear or shame; perhaps a cocktail of all three. What I saw was the Old God standing tall and dignified with his fists to his hips surveying the battlefield looking disgusted at all the so called warriors lying face down on the pavement. I could read his face and knew his thoughts...*a bunch of peacocks after all*. Then his eyes found mine and I knew that I was receiving my last and most important lesson: under any circumstance-STAND FUCKIN' TALL!!!

The police didn't shoot him. They surrounded him like a visiting dignitary. The Old God was escorted out of the yard and to the box. Truth be told, I think it was easier for the Old God to defy an enemy than to say goodbye to a son; even if, I was nothing more than a-peacock!

*   *   *

PART TWO

CHAPTER 11
DUE DILIGENCE

The first thing I sensed about the hood, as I walked through its ravaged veins, was it had become angrier. It's truly difficult to explain. Other than the uneasy and piercing feeling that since '85 the hood not only became more hostile but down right mean. Slowly, over the course of a few weeks the true culprit became more apparent. At the very heart of this chaotic whirlwind was none other than *King Crack*.

When I was in prison, *crack* was still a wild adolescent disrupting the social order; but by late '88, crack-*was the social order*; the king and all else its subjects. For me, all other hustles seemed a waste of valuable time, far too much money was being made in the distribution of this product. There were many potholes and potential pitfalls that made the odds of winning appear flimsier than the lotto. Yet like lotto, the pay off could be gigantic. Consequently, I took my time before committing myself to a definitive course of action. Like a spectator, I allowed myself to enjoy the game from the sidelines. For five months I studied a game riskier than Russian Roulette until finally convincing myself that I had figured out the formula for success. I accepted an offer of partnership from my man *Champ*.

Throughout the years, many in the streets speculated on Champ's motives for bringing me in as his bona-fide partner. Essentially, they could not figure out why someone like Champ, already firmly established, would take on a partner. The answer, though obvious, always seemed to pale in comparison to the colossal tales of dark magic and kidnapping that would make *Dean Koontz* cringe.

To this day, I am still truly mystified by the reputation, tales and anecdotes my name alone conjures. In truth, the partnership between Champ and I was the wisest business decision he could have made at the time. Champ was always a master at projecting an image of security and strength. Yet the reality was Champ brought me on to stop the pending implosion he was wise enough to spot.

Five years my senior, Champ was a contemporary of Knee. In fact, he and Knee were the best of friends in grade school. However, by the beginning of JHS, Knee grew too damned wild for Champ's taste and they drifted apart. Champ's pops put him in a boxing program to keep him off the streets and away from kids like Knee. While J.B., Knee and I were running from heroes and cops, Champ was dazzling the *Golden Gloves Circuit,* even traveling to Switzerland as a child prodigy. He even received, for a few months, private tutoring until he returned to the States.

Instead of preparing for the '84 tryouts to the Olympics, he decided to go pro. Immediately he began to climb the ranks along with a few other well known young N.Y. fighters. Champ was well on his way to a major payday. During this time, Knee and Champ rekindled their friendship. Champ kept trying to get Knee to give up the streets, but Knee was already too far gone to pull out. However, he would never simply tell Champ *no*; always sticking to his favorite *I gotta think about it* line. Champ was one of the very few dudes Knee truly liked and respected as an equal.

Somewhere around '85, Champ's light began to dim. He suffered two losses by K.O. to opponents he should have demolished. He was still young and a come back would have been possible. If only crack wasn't the cause of his downfall. No promoter would touch him by the time I left the streets. Instead of being one step away from a title fight, Champ was one step away from sleeping in abandoned buildings.

However, true to his nickname, Champ bounced back defeating his biggest opponent-King Crack in a padded cell rematch. Unfortunately, Champ's days as a professional fighter passed him by, but his warrior spirit quickly found a new arena to shine. For two years, Champ owned and operated two lucrative crack operations in Brooklyn and Queens.

I've often wondered why most of the successful drug dealers were individuals who at one time were addicts. I mean it just always puzzled me how a person devastated by a thing could in turn numb their conscience enough to devastate others. Perhaps that question nagged at me because inherent in the answer was a warning, a revelation into the inner workings of Champ. Greed and naivety limited my view. All I saw was the money.

To me Champ's weakness was he never was truly battle tested. Fist fighting was one thing, letting bullets fly was another. His own lieutenants began to suspect him of not possessing that killer instinct. Their disobedience and plotting were beginning to surface. With a reputation far exceeding my true worth at the time, bringing me aboard as a partner, gave Champ a street authenticity he badly needed. My job was to put the organization in order. Champ's was to make sure we stayed on course.

My first day on the job I called a team meeting. Initially Champ objected to shutting both operations down simultaneously, insisting that time was money and we didn't have time to waste. I stood my ground. I watched way too many gangsta flicks to doubt the success of my sit down. I wanted all the soldiers to meet their new boss. I was prepared to dismiss or kill on the spot the first one of them to have the balls to object. Prison taught me one of many valuable lessons. That amongst crooks, there was no room for weakness. No hesitation could be detected in your eyes or posture.

In no time I took command of the day-to-day operations. It appeared that Champ had been functioning as chief, in name only. Many of his workers were side dealing; using his spots to push their own product. I arrived in the nick of time and was able to cauterize the wounds. Immediately I began to make examples of those engaged in unacceptable activities. I gun butted one lieutenant unconscious and made another suck on the barrel of my new .44 Bulldog, while breaking both hands of a worker with sticky fingers. These examples were made in the first five days of my ascension. The grind was in me and my energy became infectious to all our workers. It was time to make some real money-to stop playing the game for punishment and pain.

The competition was scarce, thanks to the Police Department's *Tactical Narcotic Team*. NYC was under siege by the police who were given the green light to win the war on drugs at any cost. It was not uncommon for the TNT to plant drugs on people whose only crime was hanging out on the wrong corner or in front of the wrong building. For many hustlers, this pressure, forced them to take their show on the road. By droves, they left NYC in search of greener pastures heading to easier markets in the north and south. Only the established stayed put, determined to ride out the storm.

    We were established enough to take the occasional random hits, but not firm enough to withstand a concentrated one. I felt that my job was to ensure that no matter what, the money, like oil, must flow at all costs. Along with monitoring the two spots in Queens and Brooklyn 24/7, I also began searching for new spots to pioneer. I was patient and picky, determined to find a spot ideal in its location and potential. Through due diligence I found one.

    The Lower East Side of Manhattan, known as L.E.S., was the hood of choice. A bunch of petty tuffs roamed the hood ill prepared for the force I was about to bring. The crack head whose apartment we were going to be hustling out of lived on that block her entire life. She knew everyone and through her, so would we.

    Not to sound too political but the parallels of colonialism-that is, one country controlling and exploiting the resources of another-can be seen more clearly if you study the hustle. The invader, if he did his homework correctly, always starts off with the upper hand. The country or hood being invaded is at a disadvantage because they have no place to retreat. Everything they love, own and cherish is exposed and rendered vulnerable to the invader. The country or hood caves in and surrenders to the invader's agenda.

    So many dudes who went *out of town* to make money wound up making the *colonizer's mistake*. They allowed their greed to overrule everything else. They went to D.C., Maryland, Philadelphia, Virginia, Ohio, the Carolinas and upstate N.Y. disrespecting the cultures. Initially, they had the advantage but after time they became the enemy that unified the whole hood or town against them and in many cases, the local police and court system as well.

NYC kats began to get crucified out of town by local dudes who were tired of being disrespected and violated. By the local chicks left behind, used, abandoned and in some instances pregnant. By the local police who were tired of falling for the big city tricks and by the judges dutifully following the will of the politician who wanted to restore trust in the institutions.

I was determined not to make the colonizer's mistake in the L.E.S. About a week after we opened up shop, I began my campaign to win the hood over. I gave the youngsters on the block money to play video games or buy candy. I instructed all my workers to lend a helping hand to anyone on the block from offering to help carry groceries to buying them. We were not there to disrespect or embarrass anyone. Our goal was to make money and cause very little discomfort in the process.

I personally began recruiting the local dudes to joint the team. The method to the madness was this: the old nosey lady who sits in her window all day is less likely to call or cooperate with the pigs if it is her son, or neighbor's son she witnesses doing dirt. Every other week I changed up the faces of my lieutenants, bringing them from Brooklyn and Queens, giving the appearance of having an army at my disposal if needed. By keeping deliveries and pickups unpredictable eliminated patterns from forming. Stick up kids, such as myself; look for patterns that could be exploited to their advantage. The only pattern I wanted to matter was the high return on my investment. While the Brooklyn and Queens operations were systems I inherited, the L.E.S. operation was truly my pet project. Immediately, I sent off a couple of big faces to my team behind the wall.

Did I mention that when I arrived home I had no idea how to drive a car? Word! I bought a used '86 Honda from a car dealership, and Alicia drove it off the lot. Everyday she would give me driving lessons and in no time I became a fairly decent driver. I enjoyed spending those moments with Alicia. Seeing her frustration at my inability to park a car correctly gave way to sudden bursts of laughter at my gangsta lean behind the wheel. She would say that the only thing I mastered so far was the pose.

Both our schedules were hectic. Alicia was in college pursuing her dream, while I was on the block pursuing mine. Somehow we made time to share ourselves with one another, but I knew Alicia wanted more. She was afraid my activities were going to send me back to prison or worse - a coffin. She would tell me she was scared and in my young mind I failed to translate what she was really saying. She was confused and already contemplating a break up. Her heart told her to stay by my side. Her head told her it was time to move on.

She was striving to become a doctor; someone who was interested in healing the human body-while my profession and interests were completely the opposite. One vial at a time I sold death disguised as pleasure. What made the web even stickier was it was my occupation that paid the bills. I became her financial crutch, leaving her to concentrate on her studies. So in her heart she may have been adverse to the means, yet it was the ends that ensnared her. But for how long? I couldn't help but wonder.

*   *   *

CHAPTER 12
SECURING THE BORDERS

The Q-Club, a popular social club in Queens, was the place of worship one particular night for some major peacocks and their underlings. A Black Tie Affair was the protocol. The party was for a low-key baller out of Far Rockaway named *Fats*. He decided to spend his thirtieth birthday in the limelight. My attendance proved a pricey move because I was able to meet a couple of kats that would prove valuable down the line. With the Moet and Dom Pérignon being consumed at a rate almost equaling the amount of cocaine snorted, I was surprised a party atmosphere was being maintained. Bottles, the expensive kind, were being popped throughout the club giving off the sound of random shots being fired. With so many inflated egos in one location I just knew at any minute, the drama would start but it didn't.

I was chillin' in the back room, where a small constellation of ghetto superstars gathered, observing a high stakes game of poker. *Fats*, his right hand man *A.D.*, a couple of other kats and Champ were all locked into the game of chance. As prearranged I sat next to an official live wire out of Harlem named *Dice*, a light skinned Buddha with a jovial smile and even white teeth. He was a friend of Jah-Loyal and his brother Bad. We hit it off immediately and in very little time our communication turned to business.

In my opinion Champ had grown way too dependent on a creepy Colombian dude named *Jorge*. Champ's argument was that Jorge supplied the best quality of fish scale in the five boroughs. Fish scale, while not the best kind of cocaine to snort, was definitely the best strain of coke to add water and baking soda to. My beef was that Jorge was an overextended hustler. Far too many dudes were dealing with him for my tastes. For the police not to be aware of his presence, was just too naïve to assume.

Then there was the issue of character-he was a worm, slithery in every way. He spoke with double meanings and always seemed to be scheming; the type that never looks you in the eye preferring to set his sights on something behind you. It felt like every transaction we made with him might be the one where the goons emerge out of closets or from behind closed doors, turning a simple drug deal into a robbery and then a homicide. I was thirsty to catch the earthworm first. I even went so far as to suggest that we use him as live bait to catch some bigger fish, you know, utilize the worm the right way, but Champ adamantly refused to even discuss the issue. He trusted Jorge unconditionally-he considered him a friend.

    I refused to warm to the joker and that's why I was politicking with Dice. Dice was supplying heavy weight to a small circle of friends; at least that's what he called them. By keeping his circle small he was able to avoid the pitfalls so many other of his competitors found themselves in. Dice appeared sincere when he welcomed me into his circle of friends. I believed it was Jah's vouching for my character that relaxed his caution. Even from the federal penitentiary, Bad and Jah still exerted tremendous pull in Harlem.

    After the party I told Champ of the connection I made for us while he was busy losing his money. Champ seemed disinterested and unimpressed. In his opinion, there was nothing wrong with Jorge and so we decided to let the matter die.

    Several months after the party, Jorge told Champ that he was having a *Winter Clearance Sale* claiming he was making way for a new shipment by getting rid of the old. Since Champ was his man he was going to give us ten keys for $140 grand. It was a deal that seemed too good to be true. I was skeptical of the deal and told Champ so.

    "Come on Kay…he's giving us three bricks free."
Champ was attempting to reason with me.
    "Why?"
    "Fuck you mean 'why'…you can't be serious. Does it matter why?"
    "Yeah it matters-he never gives us any play. We pay for 1000 grams, best believe we get 990. That nigga includes the rubber and duct tape it's wrapped in. Now

> *all of a sudden he wants to bless us-nah Champ something ain't right."*
> *"Something ain't right? Like what Kay? Like what?"*
> *"I don't know. The quality might be half ass or straight junk."*

Champ, his right hand man *Divine* and I were sitting in his Benz speeding down the FDR on our way to a hole in the wall hamburger spot in Harlem called *Willie Burgers*. It had been a long day and so I was talking to him reclined in the passenger seat with my eyes shut.

> *"Why now? Unfuckin' believable Kay...it's a golden opportunity and you're questioning why. Because golden opportunities come once in a blue moon, so when the moon turns blue-we jump on the opportunity. Is that philosophical enough for you? 'Why this, why that?' I keep telling you this Plato and Aristotle shit don't work in the real world. That's that prison shit and in case it hasn't dawned on you my man, you are not in the big yard anymore."*

Throughout this entire exchange Divine remained silent.

> *"Look Rocky Balboa..."*

...a name that always got Champ tight...

> *"...all I'm saying is that it doesn't fit Jorge's pattern. He's a stingy muthafucka and three free keys from that creep is beyond generous."*

Even with my eyes closed I knew Champ was looking in his rearview-catching eye contact with Divine. They were so secretive and inseparable that I began to suspect that they might actually be lovers.

> *"It doesn't fit the pattern? Are you serious? Fuck are you a criminal psychologist tracking serial killers? You hear this shit Divine? This the type of shit I gotta put up with. 'It doesn't fit the pattern...it doesn't fit the pattern'."*

Champ was repeating my words to himself as if by doing so would bring him closer to comprehending my point.

> *"Fuck are you a seamstress or something? Talking this pattern shit."*

Champ struck a nerve with that one.

> "Yo…I don't trust the slime ball-he thinks he's smarter than us and…"

Champ cut me off.

> "See…see that's it right there. That's really what this is all about. You don't like son. You never liked him because he don't recognize Big Bad Kay. I keep telling you this ain't Boy Scouts. This is business-dollars and cents. It's not about liking muthafuckas
> it's about doing business. You can't make business decisions based on emotions."

Champ had heard enough. He was pulling rank.

> "Look nigga…it's a done deal. For the next couple of days collect the money from the spots-nobody gets paid. It's a sacrifice for the whole team; including you. We need another thirty grand to put with the rest of the re-up money and I'm not about to come out of my own pocket."

I had over fifty grand saved and could have easily put up the thirty, but it would have been an investment in a deal my instincts were against. Perhaps I still had a lot to learn.

Instructing me to tax the entire team was a crafty move by Champ. I would look like the bad guy and when the grumbling started I would be the cause of the complaints. As if Jimmy Hoffa was resurrected, Champ would then come to the disgruntled workers' rescue. It was a power play designed to weaken my integrity in the eyes of the team. Clearly the scheming begins when you stop paying people for their services; but hey, it was Champ's call. We were partners in theory but in truth it was still homeboy's show. Like a good soldier, though disagreeing with the directive, I followed orders. It was a matter of protocol and without protocol, chaos would be king.

Mercilessly, I kept the team on a military grind determined to reach the quota as quickly as possible. I knew that time was against me. Everyday the workers worked for free would eventually become one more scheme I would have to foil. My efforts paid off and in 2 ½ days we had our money and my part of the operation was done.

Jorge owned a bodega store right off of Broadway in the Williamsburg section of Brooklyn. The store was nothing but a front for all of Jorge's transactions. I gave Champ the money and the rest was on him. He left to go meet Jorge at the store while I decided to take Alicia to Red Lobster.

I picked Alicia up from school and hit the highway heading toward Long Island. The sun had just begun to set when my beeper began vibrating. I looked at the number and code. The number was unfamiliar but the code belonged to Divine. I knew that he had gone with Champ and so I figured the beep must be important. It took me a few minutes to find a pay phone that was working

"*Yo...*"

Divine answered on the first ring.

"*Yo...where's Champ?*"

He asked me this like I was supposed to know.

"*He 'pose to be with you.*" I replied.

"*Yeah...he left us here to collect the product-Niecy beeped him and he went running.*"

"*So what. Did the deal go down?*" I asked.

"*Yeah...yeah. Champ gave Jorge the dough, Jorge counted it and then told us to hang out. He had to go get the product.*"

"*Ayat...so what's wrong?*"

"*What's wrong? It's been over three hours and the joker is not back yet.*"

"*He left you in the store for three hours?*"

"*Nah...the store was closed. He said something about it being renovated and shit. We're in one of his apartments.*"

"*Apartments...?*"

"*And Champ is with Niecy?*"

"*Yup...we chillin' in Jorge's crib waiting on him. His baby moms and little son is here with us.*"

"*Niecy, not answering the phone or the beep? Where's this apartment at?*" I inquired.

"*We're over here on Schaefer between Evergreen and Broadway.*"

111

"Ayat check it...stay put. I'm gonna swing around to Niecy's crib and see what's up. Let's hope nothing happened to Jorge."
"...Or our money."
"Definitely that...who's with you?"
"Rick is here with me-he's a real family man. He's in the next room playing video games with the little kid. Jorge's baby moms is acting like she wanna give Rick some pussy and shit."
"Nah...nah...make sure that shit don't happen."
"C'mon Kay...you think I'm stupid...death before dishonor baby. I know the code."
"Yeah...but Rick thinks he's a fuckin' pretty boy so make sure he don't try to slide her a number or something. The last thing we need is a ruined connect."
"Don't sweat it. I got it under control."
"Make sure you do."

I broke the connection. After explaining to Alicia the slight change of plans I hit the expressway. Niecy lived in Starrett City, about a thirty minute ride, so I put my foot on the gas and drove in silence. Alicia was listening to her *Babyface* cassette-singing *Whip Appeal* out loud. Her beautiful voice acted as a calming agent, giving me the opportunity to contemplate.

What the hell was Jorge thinking leaving dudes around his family? If that wasn't a sign of slipping I didn't know what was. But he wasn't the only fool slipping-what the hell was on Champ's mind? How in the world do you leave a job undone? In the middle of a campaign, the General just ups and leaves-in hot pursuit of a skirt? Baffling. The worse case scenario was Jorge got knocked or robbed; either scenario was too disastrous to think about for too long and so I tried to push the possibility out of my mind.

I reached Niecy's crib only to discover Champ was no longer there. I missed him by minutes. According to Niecy, as soon as Champ turned on his beeper-Divine got through. Champ was on his way back to Jorge's apartment. I beeped him from

Niecy's crib using my code but he failed to call back. I laughed to myself because I knew he wouldn't. This shit was shaping up to look like a disaster and the last thing he wanted to hear from me was *I told you so*. Oh well...I decided to let him stress out over this shit; I had a date with my lady and I already wasted enough time on Champ's 'blue moons' and 'golden opportunities.'

Back on the highway, heading toward a shrimp scampi platter, my mind was racing. Alicia was in the driver's seat weaving her way through the light traffic with grace. The criminal minded tape held our attention when the thought hit me. Divine and Rick were sitting in Jorge's apartment like lame ducks. *Fuck!* Praying I was wrong, but suspecting I wasn't, I told Alicia to get off the highway. We had to find a pay phone-fast. I was thinking if Jorge had gotten robbed he might try to trade his life for Champ's, Divine's and Rick's. The thieves thinking that there could be a lot more money stashed somewhere could really catch them off guard and punish them.

We were in the LeFrak section of Queens when I finally found a pay phone that worked. I dialed the phone number that Divine beeped me from earlier. After a series of rings the phone was answered.

"*Yeah...*"

A muffled voice responded.

"*Divine...that you?*"

"*Ahhha...*"

Again muffled.

"*Did he get there yet?*"

"*Yeah.*"

Something was wrong-he wasn't talking.

"*Say something nigga. This 'yeah' shit is spooking me.*"

"*Like what...?*"

I was baffled. The voice didn't belong to Divine-I broke the connection. Against her indignant protest I hailed a cab for Alicia, I was sending her home, out of harm's way.

"*Kameek...tell me what's going on.*"

"*Not now Alicia-get in the cab.*"

"*Why do you always do this Kameek?*"

"Do what Alicia?"
"Shut me out!"
I was growing impatient. Valuable time was being wasted.
"Alicia...chill out and get in the cab."
"Kameek...I asked you a question."
"WHAT? What the fuck is your question?"
Her eyes began to water, her feelings were hurt, but in war there's always casualties and if it was her feelings over my comrades lives-then hey-emotional scars build character.
"Why do you always shut me out of your world?"
"Because it's dark. Alicia it's dark."
"Maybe I'm not afraid of the dark."
"Yeah...'cause you never been in it."
Gently I grabbed her arm trying to guide her into the back seat of the taxi. She became irate.
"Get the hell off me! Don't fuckin' touch me!"
She pulled away from me and got in the cab. I kept my composure, closed the door, handed the driver a twenty and began reciting my address. Alicia cut me off in mid-sentence and gave the cabbie her mother's address. As the cab pulled off Alicia kept her gaze straight ahead not once looking my way. That little gesture of hers hit its mark. I was hurt but what could I do? It was as if I was caught in two opposing worlds, contradictory realities both fighting for dominion. Alicia was my - salvation, the streets my - curse. I cursed my luck and stuck to the code.

Back then I had a primitive stash in my car; nothing that could withstand a thorough police search yet slick enough to get me through a routine traffic stop. I pulled my seventeen shot 9mm Taurus out of the stash and headed toward Bushwick. I had no plan of action, I wasn't sure of the building; all I knew was the block. I told myself something would give - it had to.

As soon as I turned onto Schaefer my heart stopped for what felt like an eternity. Like an owl my eyes grew wide in suspense, too fuckin' late to turn around I was heading directly into the eye of the storm. Marked and unmarked cop cars were on one side of the street while plain clothed and uniformed cops stood on the other. Though nighttime, the entire block was illuminated by powerful spotlights. The two cars in front of me were moving at a snail's pace causing a torrent of curses to escape my lips.

Slowly I drove through the enemy's gauntlet - trying to keep my game face from exposing the dread I felt. A primal fear; the paralyzing type that freezes your thinking allowing only instincts to rule; I was preparing myself for the bang out - refusing to ever again allow myself to be locked inside a cage. If stopped there could be only one of two outcomes - escape or death; the true meaning of ride or die.

Sharp as a razor the realization of my predicament calmed me - it was a waiting game that intensified with every slow inch my car took. Alicia came to mind, a stab of regret pierced my armor; wishing we hadn't parted the way we had. Hoping that I would see her again, painstakingly, I trudged on. At one point my imagination got the better of me and I saw my mother, brother and Alicia standing over my casket crying. J.B. was handcuffed in prison garb looking at the monster he thought he created; a frightening vision or perhaps an omen? Fortunately that day hadn't arrived.

Blessed be the gods, the attention of the police was on more serious matters. I made it through without so much as a second glance. I got out of dodge with the quickness. Common sense overrode my curiosity and I headed home. Ten minutes into my trip I received another beep - it was Champ. He picked up yelling...

"Fuck, fuck...something's wrong Kay-something went wrong."

Champ was stating the obvious.

"Five-o knocked Divine and Rick."

"Calm down...what happened?"

"I don't have a fuckin' clue. When I got there the police were dragging Rick and Divine out in cuffs."

"That's it?"

"What do you mean 'that's it'? C'mon Kay...not now. Don't start that philosophy bullshit now."

I was tired of giving Champ the wrong impression of who he was really dealing with.

"Look nigga...you're the clown who orchestrated this disaster so stop acting like a fuckin' bitch. Being arrested is better than being dead. Call Goldberg or whatever that muthafucka's name is that you always bragging about. Wake that fucka up if you have to and send him to the precinct to represent his clients. This way we will find out what's going on while making sure dem boys don't get diarrhea of the mouth."

"Divine won't tell."

Champ couldn't resist that silly ass comment.

"What the fuck is he? Your lover or something? Get a grip and send that mouthpiece down there before Divine disappoints you."

Champ held his tongue. Perhaps I hit the bulls-eye with that lover shit after all. I continued...

"I'll call you in the morning to find out the 411 but 'til then hold your fuckin' head-it's no time to panic."

"Yeah man...you're right. I'm on top of it-I needed the chin check partner."

I hung up on him. No matter the outcome of this fiasco, I told myself that from this day forward, the balance of power between Champ and I had shifted. If my life was going to be placed on the line it would be because of my own choices. We were cut from two very different cloths. Like Bounty and Charmin - both looked the same but only one could absorb the spill without tearing.

The following morning the ring of the phone interrupted my sleep. I was in bed alone. For the first time in weeks Alicia was not by my side. I was hoping that the person on the other end of the line was her, but knew it wasn't because the tone of the ring was sinister. A bearer of bad news was on the other end of the line. Before answering it I took time to gain my composure.

"Yeah...it's me Champ."

Like I said, a bearer of bad news.

"Spit it."

"Man Kay...it was all a set up from the very beginning. The nigga Jorge did us dirty. It was a scam Kay. There

never were ten keys. The joker called the police and told them that three dudes were holding his wife and child hostage."

"Wow..."

Was the only response I could muster.

"Yeah...who you telling, and the bitch was down with it. She's claiming they threatened to rape and kill her in front of her son if her husband didn't cooperate."

"Cooperate how?"

"Man we have no idea. Goldberg couldn't get anything out of the D.A. or the police."

"So where's Jorge?" "No idea. I'm assuming that he and his bitch is under some kind of protection."

"So are they looking for you?"

"I'm not sure. Goldberg didn't mention it..."

I cut him off with this thought.

"You know Jorge intended for you to get trapped off-don't you?"

I wanted to rub the point in.

"Yeah...I mean it's obvious I was the target-luckily Niecy called and needed me to take care of something for her."

Lucky or coincidental...

"Hey...thank God for Niecy," I said, not sure if I had masked the sarcasm.

"But Kay for the life of me, I can't figure out why this nigga Jorge would go out like this."

It was a sucka vic question. Champ sounded like a tourist who just got ripped off in midtown by a wino.

"Because this is a game of predator and prey. The stakes are always perilous. You can't figure out why a snake moves the way it does-the key is to recognize and accept the snake for what it is. Kill, or avoid it-but never try to befriend or reform it."

"What's that? One of those verses from the O.G. Bible?"

"Nah...Socrates," I shot back.

"Ha, ha...that's cute Kay. That's cute."

"Nah nigga...it's gritty-with me it's always gritty."

A chasm of silence erupted between us. The static from the phone grew louder in its intensity by the second. Finally Champ found his way to the reason for his call.

"Yeah...yo...check it Kay. I'm gonna lay low for a few days-just to play it safe, ya dig. Ima need you to hold the fort down."

I was far from surprised. The timidity in his voice told me he was rattled. I had no problem with taking total control of the operation. In fact, that had been my plan all along but I couldn't let the sucka off the hook so easy.

"Psst, man...the workers haven't been paid in four days, we have very little product left, our supplier just geeked us out of our re – up money, we got two lawyers who gotta get paid, bail money that needs to be raised and your talking about laying low?"

"Look muthafucka...are you gonna take care of things or not?"

"Hey...I have no choice. It's either that or the ship sinks---right or wrong?"

Champ ignored my bleak assessment.

"Good. I'll check back with you in about a week."

And with that the line went dead.

   *   *   *

CHAPTER 13
SECURING THE BORDERS

First move...secure a new connect. After about seven attempts I finally got through to Dice. He seemed pleased to hear from me and eager to do business. We arranged to meet that night in Harlem at a restaurant called *Sylvia's*.

That had been the easy part. The difficulty would be in facing the workers with another sad song and dance about taking one for the team and why they wouldn't get paid another day. Already, a handful of good workers quit; while another worker, a clown named *Green Eyes*, ran off with a $1000 package. Like cancer, word quickly spread about the Divine and Rick situation and I could bet that some of the remaining workers were preparing strategic exits as well. I'm a firm believer that no problem can withstand the assault of sustained thinking for too long and the more I thought about the situation the more clear the solution became.

I decided to pay all the workers what we owed them out of my own stash. For me it was a matter of loyalty, for they were the ones who endured the daily hazards of the hustle; the ones on the front line taking the bulk of the risk. They had to be paid even if it had to come out of my own pocket.

Boy was they happy. The rejuvenated look in their eyes confirmed my decision. It was a morale boost for everyone, though it was my money being depleted. I knew that the amount was peanuts compared to my purchase. The look in their eyes assured me that I had gained their confidence-the first step toward loyalty. I made sure they knew that it was my decision to pay them and that Champ decided to lay low for a while. Champ's power play backfired and instead of alienating me from the workers, his plan brought me closer to them.

I drove to Sylvia's with Handbone in the passenger seat. Since the day I came home, Handbone had been doing odd and end jobs for me. He was no longer a drunk. He claimed to have found a new lease on life the day of my shooting. As you recall it was Handbone who stood over me and staunched my bleeding.

He also took the gun from me-saving me from catching a gun charge. A trained soldier, a survivor of the war in Vietnam, was now my unseen hand. Our reserved table stood next to the window facing the street, providing all at the table a bird's eye view of our immediate surroundings. *What a clever location for our first meeting.* Seated at the table across from Handbone and me were Dice, his right hand man *Preme* and another kat named *Sam*. It was Sam who caught my attention. Immediately I knew Sam for what he was-the enforcer. His body language spoke of danger masked in a façade of peace and tranquility. Though poised and serene I could tell that his true self was coiled and ready for any sign of danger.

To the untrained eye his calm demeanor could fool you into a false sense of security. His graying hair and resigned facial lines gave him the appearance of being in his late forties or early fifties. But it was his eyes that bespoke of a seasoned confidence of imminent danger that the rest of him convincingly concealed. Sam was a cold-blooded killer. His presence reminding me, once more, that I was in a big boy's league whose slogan *come correct or don't come at all* was law. As I looked at the three faces before me I couldn't help but wonder, as they looked at Handbone, if they could see the same coiling in his eyes as I saw in Sam's. When they nodded at him as a fellow colleague I had my answer.

Dice knew all the waiters by their first names and they all seemed anxious to serve our table; obviously Dice was a big tipper. After a few minutes of small talk a beautiful sister by the name of *Jamilla* took our orders. We pretty much ate in silence with the only distraction being Preme excusing himself every ten minutes to answer his beeps. The conversation began in earnest when the table was cleared and we awaited the dessert.

"*You know Kay...*", Dice began, "*I was wondering when you was gonna give a fellah a call. When I didn't hear from you right away I began asking around about you. I needed to know more than what Jah-Loyal told me. I mean don't take this the wrong way but it was Jah's word that eventually took his team down.*"

HONOR amongst THIEVES

He was referring to Jah's vouching for Trey. I held my tongue not wanting to sound too desperate but the truth of the matter-I was. The spots were running on fumes and if it meant standing here and listening to this philosophical crap then it was a necessary evil I had to endure. He continued...

> "Jah was always a hot head. I remember one time Jah went to check his man in St. Nick Projects. When he knocked on his man's door-Jah's girlfriend at the time answered the door in a bathrobe. With not one word said Jah stormed into the house and shot his man in the belly."

Dice paused long enough to see my response. Sam lit a cigarette anxiously awaiting my outlook as well. Just hearing the story I could feel the rage and betrayal Jah must've felt. Imagining I was Jah and Alicia was the girl in the bathrobe, I responded...

> "Yeah...homeboy was lucky it was only a gut shot."

Sam blew out a chimney of pent up smoke. Dice was shaking his head letting me know I gave the wrong answer.

> "The girl in the robe was Jah's girl but she was also his man's cousin. Since she was really nothing but a piece of pussy to Jah, another one of his possessions, he never took the time to find out anything about her-especially something so petty as to who she was or might not be related to. My point Kay, is that Jah was always quick to draw conclusions based on distorted or limited facts. His man lived but their friendship didn't-in fact he became one of Jah's most bitter enemies.
>
> I warned Bad long ago that Jah's decision making process was faulty-but you know how that goes-that's his little brother so he overlooked the obvious and it cost him dearly. I say all of this to say that many crews and hustlers have fallen because they overlooked the flaws. They placed their trust in instincts and not logic. They move first and think second. I may not look it but I just turned thirty-six four days ago. I've been in this game for twenty-one years and I have never been to jail for more than three days. Now there's only two

> *ways I could have avoided prison this long. Either I'ma snitch or a muthafuckin' genius. I ain't no snitch so I must be a rocket scientist."*

Sam cracked a gapped tooth smile while Handbone lit a cigarette-the two killers studying each others endless spirals of smoke, as if the smoke itself carried some coded message that kept eluding them.

> *"So what does all this have to do with me?"*

It was a rhetorical question designed to get him back into talking. Dice was smiling but his eyes were weighing carefully. He still hadn't made up his mind regarding me. He resumed his train of thought...

> *"Everyone I asked told me you are a hot head-a thief at heart."*

The way he said it stung-but I held my tongue.

> *"...that if you could steal sweet from sugar you would. Word is that you went up against a big dog and though he bit you pretty hard, you held your own. Strangely, he died the very day you got sentenced."*

Like a chubby Sherlock Holmes, Dice looked directly at Handbone as if he figured out who killed Smooth and Smiley. I almost laughed. Did this nigga really call himself a genius a minute earlier?

> *"Kay, I'm gonna be honest with you. If you were hustling here in Harlem I would have absolutely nothing to do with you. Harlem has a unique tradition; the man who gave me my first break knew me since I was a baby. Shit...he knew my mama and papa since they were little. So he knew what I was made of because he watched and more importantly helped mold me. That's the Harlem tradition. Tradition in Harlem says that a man making money not only feeds his family, but his neighborhood as well. You gotta give back. Tradition in Harlem says that if a man dies or goes to prison, his son can inherit his throne and continue to feed the family. That's not the case in Brooklyn. In Brooklyn, if the father dies or goes to prison, the wolves would kill the son and if they could fuck the mother."*

"What you tryin' to say? We don't have honor?" I challenged.

"Not honor-sound tradition. We all have traditions that are unique to our environment. Brooklyn's tradition is only the ruthless survive-a cutthroat-dog eat dog vibe. My point being not which borough is better, that's for kids and rappers to discuss-not men. I'm just trying to highlight the differences. That wild gung-ho gangsta type has no place in Harlem. Yeah we have a few young mavericks running around but they won't last long-they never do. But in Brooklyn the more violent the reputation the less opposition you will encounter. Brooklyn is a goddamn city in itself and I've been itching to tap its reservoir. I plan on retiring when I'm forty and if I can expand my tentacles to Brooklyn and Queens for the next four years, my retirement will be all that I dreamt of. So I'm willing to gamble. I'm willing to invest in you Kay and your potential."

"Because I'm violent?"

"Because of your violent reputation-there's a difference."

He paused again to see if I understood his meaning. I did and so I allowed him to continue...

"Here are the rules-I will only deal with you or him," he said, pointing his finger at Handbone.

"That's it. No one is to even know I exist. Is this a deal?"

I couldn't help but nod my head like a six year old being asked would he like a Mr. Softee ice cream cone.

"Secondly, I don't deal with nickel and dime shit. Every time you call me I'm expecting you to want at least five and better-ten is more to my liking."

My bubble quickly burst. I only had enough for one kilo. Dice must've sensed my mood change.

"What's wrong?"

I didn't want to tell him but my hand was forced.

"Man...we just took a major loss-I took everything I could scrounge to come cop something from you."

Dice didn't even blink.
> "How much you got?"
>
> "Enough for a key."

Preme turned his head toward Dice to see if this dilemma put a wrinkle in Dice's plans. Like I said Dice didn't blink.
> "Where's the money?"
>
> "In the trunk of my car."
>
> "Ayat...give Sam the car keys."

I handed the keys over. Dice then turned to Sam and said...
> "Put three fishes in the trunk."

Sam immediately left the table. Dice studied me once more and then almost as an after thought spoke...
> *"I'm gonna give you two bricks on consignment-I don't expect you to pay me for those two fishes until you can buy ten. When you are ready to buy ten, make sure there's an extra fifty grand in it for the two I'm giving you now. Also, the very next buy I'm expecting you to take nothing less than five off my hands. Deal?"*
>
> *"Deal!"*

As if it was all staged Jamilla appeared out of nowhere with the dessert. I let out a sigh of relief. This thing was working out better than I could've imagined. Call me *Curious George* or whatever but I had a question for the genius that needed answering.
> *"Dice...if I'm a thief at heart, why give me two bricks on consignment?"*

Dice smiled.
> *"Believe me Kay I do my homework and truthfully, two kilos are mere trinkets to me. If you run off with something so small it would be a minor loss for me; a small price to pay to find out if you are worthy of membership to my small circle of friends."*

His use of the word *trinket* let me know he had spoken with Jah about the chain fiasco on Rikers. It was Jah who placed the five grand in my hand to see my reaction. The two extra keys was Dice's way of testing me. Dice continued to hammer home his point.

> "*Besides, I know where all three of your spots are and a great deal more.*"

I knew at some point a veiled threat would be given. I smiled and so did he. He smiled at the smoothness in which he delivered his threat. I smiled because little did the genius know he wasn't the only one who had done his homework.

*   *   *

CHAPTER 14
LOOSE ENDS

Despite securing the new connect the following weeks were still hectic. Champ was dead serious about his laying low crap. In fact the only time he showed his face was when it was time to collect his share of the profits.

Then, like a pimple, a new problem emerged. Both Divine and Rick no longer trusted Champ. They considered him suspect. Niecy, just happened to call with a dire emergency and Champ's leaving in the nick of time was just too convenient for them. To make matters worse, Champ made no effort to go visit them while they were being held at the Brooklyn House of Detention, even though he lived less than six blocks away. While I was not comfortable with the entire way things were going down I wasn't ready to label Champ suspect, primarily because I couldn't see a motive.

Add to that the fact, we weren't the only kats Jorge played the shit out of. When the smoke cleared we discovered that entire week, Jorge was conning hustlers out of their money with that *Winter Clearance Sale* nonsense. He sold one crew seven kilos of sheet rock and baking soda, while another crew lost their money with nothing to hold but a promise. Nevertheless, it became sadistically obvious that he saved his best *fuck you clown* performance for Champ.

Jorge, sold his store about a month earlier, but the owners gave him three weeks to get his affairs in order. Unfortunately, dudes weren't convinced that he sold the store, so it went up in flames on the night of its new owner's grand opening. Jorge left the game behind-at least in N.Y.C., because there was nowhere in the city that he would be safe. I figured he skipped town, probably heading back to Colombia. I was convinced Jorge would never be seen again.

So what could Champ's motive be for setting up his own team for failure, especially when he owned the franchise? I had to concede that his behavior as of late created more questions than answers. In this game, a person must be transparent when dealing with his teammates. When you move suspiciously you become a suspect. Divine and Rick refused the lawyers Champ had for them. It was on me to find them new counsel. They were being held without bail, which saved me the headache of trying to pay a ransom.

Despite all the drama, I did find a little recreation. I was driving down Nostrand Avenue on my way to checking on the spot in Crown Heights when I spotted the clown talking to the mailman on the corner. He looked so comfortable, so untouchable; with such nerve I knew I had to get him. I parked my car a block away, snatched my slugger and began slowly jogging toward him. About fifty paces away I began picking up speed. It wasn't until I was about ten paces away did he finally realize something wasn't what it should be. Perhaps it was the mailman's startled expression right before my Louisville Slugger smashed into the back of the creep's skull. He hit the floor harder than I expected and was out cold. The mailman took off leaving his mail carriage behind.

I robbed the sucka for the few pieces of jewelry he had on. Then I took his New Balance sneakers off his feet and threw them on top of the closest roof. Satisfied with the lesson I administered, I jogged back to the car and continued on my way. I wasn't into taking losses and though I couldn't get to Jorge because he was definitely somewhere on the other side of the border or somewhere below the equator; I'd be damned if I would've allowed green eyes to cross without paying.

Alicia was avoiding me, still upset about some sentimental shit only women find important. I didn't have the time or patience to read her mind and figure shit out. I was caught in the moment and committed to the grind, despite my feelings for her. I wasn't gonna sweat her and so I pushed her out of my mind.

I moved my moms into a duplex apartment in Queens. J.B. was five months shy of going to the parole board and all indications pointed to his return home. My mother wanted to get him away from his old surroundings and so it was the first gift she accepted from my ill-gotten gains. Both J.B. and I were happy that she did. I was heavily into the streets and having my moms still living in the hood made her an easy target for retaliation, abduction or worse. It's all about covering your bases and many hustlers made the mistake of leaving their loved ones in vulnerable situations.

I was also able to track down Knee's baby moms, *Gwen*. She was living in the boogie down struggling to raise Robert Jr. on her own. She was a good woman with a good heart, whose love for her son had become her religion. I didn't understand how Knee could fuck up his relationship with her. Then again, who was I to try to figure shit out when my own relationship was on the brink of extinction.

Gwen had no problem with allowing Knee to see his son, but under no circumstances would she be the one to take him. I respected her position. Knee was one of those abusive kats, while Gwen wasn't one of those weak-minded broads who confused abuse with love.

She and Robert Jr. were sleeping on mattresses without bed frames; their clothes were in boxes as opposed to dresser drawers. Bed sheets instead of curtains covered their windows while a coat hanger was used as an antenna for the color television. I gave Gwen $2500 to buy some furniture. I told her that as long as she allowed Knee to see his little man I would continue to assist her. She seemed relieved, not so much for her sake but for her son's. There were so many things she claimed she wanted to do for lil' man, like exposing him to karate and music lessons but never had the means to do so. Now she did.

Robert Jr., who I instantly began calling 'lil man, was five years old and full of energy, a spitting image of his Pops-in appearance and nature. I gave 'lil man a $100 bill and told him it came from his father. His eyes grew wide as he held the bill. Lovingly, his mother, rubbing the top of his head said...

"That's a whole lot a money baby. Put it in your pocket before you lose it."

With great joy 'lil man did as he was told.

"What do you say when someone gives you a gift?" Gwen asked.

"Thank you," he yelled my way.

"You're welcome, but what are you gonna do with all that money", I asked.

'Lil man's face grew serious. His eyebrows arched in deep concentration.

"I gonna buy my mummy a big-big house and I gonna buy my grandma a new car."

Barely containing her laughter, Gwen asked...

"What about daddy? You're not gonna buy him anything?"

'Lil man's head began bobbing up and down.

"I gonna, I gonna buy my daddy out of jail."

A statement made with such conviction and finality I immediately felt his longing. Memories of my own childhood and desire to see my father again surfaced. Gwen, quickly changed the subject.

"That's all you gonna buy?"

"I gonna save the rest."

"How much you gonna have left?", I asked.

'Lil man took my question seriously. Deftly, he began counting on his fingers until finally settling on a figure.

"Fifty-four dollars", he said.

I smiled...*if only life was that simple.* I entrusted *Mimmi*, a cross-eyed red bone from my block who had a crush on Knee, with the task of bringing 'lil man up to see his father every other week. You would think that seeing his little man would calm him down, but the day after his first visit, he cut a dude for looking in his cell. Knee claimed to have warned the dude three times about looking in his cell and since the dude failed to pay heed, Knee's hand was forced.

I understood the violation. Only sneak thieves case a cell, but there was also a bigger picture. Knee was prolonging his stay in prison while his son desperately needed him home. He cut the guy on principle but which principle holds more weight-a jail code or a father's pledge? I couldn't help but wonder...

I was the one who took responsibility of playing daddy to his son in his absence. I escorted 'lil man on a class trip to Sesame Place. I took him to the circus and Toys R' Us for his birthday, buying him a Nintendo game and bedroom set. It was I who 'lil man came running to whenever he saw me. It was me, but it was supposed to be Knee. And after a while, like so many other dudes in prison, Knee's *matters of principle* became nothing but convenient excuses for avoiding the truth-the character of honor is responsibility and all else is shame.

In general, prison is full of villains and creeps-but even amidst the rubble of broken men with broken dreams stands a few good men; men worthy of remembrance. I was duty bound to keep it official with them. Every money order, package, every bus ride in which I sent loved ones up to see them was my way of saying I remember.

My parole officer gave me permission to go visit J.B. He was graduating from Marist College in Green Haven Correctional Facility. Both my mother and I went and it was the first time in over six years that the three of us sat at a table and broke bread together.

J.B. earned a Bachelor Degree in Sociology and was given the honor of addressing the graduating class. I was extremely proud of him but also a little sad. Up until that point, although I knew the change was occurring, the realization of what that change meant escaped me. As I watched J.B. expertly command the stage, as I listened to him articulate his message of giving back to the community, I understood that my partner in crime was no longer my crime partner. We were on two separate paths - heading in what seemed two opposing directions.

I still recall parts of my brother's speech-especially when he began explaining his reasoning for dedicating his life to giving back.

"Why is it that Blacks and Latinos combined only make up 26% of the state's population yet comprises 85% of the prison population? How is this possible? The majority of this 85% comes from seven neighborhoods or twenty-one targeted districts in N.Y.C. alone. What is happening in the Bed-Stuys, the South Sides, South Bronxes and the Harlems of N.Y.C. and for that matter, America? Why are these particular communities sending more of us to prison than to college? Sending more of us to the grave than the

> altar? What will our future look like, our legacy, our fingerprint on the world if the majority of our doctors, lawyers, teachers, engineers, leaders, warriors and fathers are incarcerated or buried? They're building more prisons but its not for us, we are already here. These new prisons are being built for our children, for our future. If we don't break this vicious cycle who will? Can we really expect the same villain who set the trap to save us from it? Let's face it, we are an abandoned nation, a nation within a nation, and until we embrace this sense of nationhood our situation will never get better."

For the first time J.B. looked directly at me and asked...

> "We use this term live wire a lot. But what is a live wire? Who is a live wire?"

Someone in the audience yelled...

> "That's right black man! Speak the truth!"

J.B. continued...

> "Is a live wire someone who destroys his own clan-his own people by pushing poison into their veins or bullets into the brains of our future leaders? Are you a live wire because of some twisted code, or because someone, anyone, failed to walk cautiously in the presence of a live wire? Are you a live wire because you left a mother with the unbearable pain of watching her son's body scraped off the pavement like a dog, all because your reputation was at stake? I submit to you today that a live wire is none of the above. Those are all characteristics of a chump and not a man. A live wire is one who stands against the chumps and their madness; one who is determined to defend his people, his clan-no matter the consequences. A live wire is one who is in the business of producing a healthy people-in short, we are in the business of ourselves, not our destruction."

J.B. continued to speak but he was no longer looking at me. I was unable to focus on the rest of his speech because I was trying to figure out the message he was sending my way. Was he saying he was coming home to go against his own brother?

About an hour after the speech, I was able to get him alone and question him on the meaning.
"Yo J.B., correct me if I'm wrong but was that message directed at me?"
He began smiling.
"I knew you were gonna ask me that."
"Yeah well...was it meant for me or not?"
"It was a speech Kay, designed to make you do just what you are doing now."
"Which is?"
"To think. Think about the path of destruction you are on. Would I be your brother? Could I really claim to love you yet not warn you that you are on the wrong side? Look Kay, I'm grateful for the money orders, and all the other stuff you do for me, but I know that the Law of Karma can't favor you forever. I don't want to come home, only to start visiting you in prison or worse, a graveyard."
"Yeah, yeah I read your letters, but the part about defending your people-your clan no matter the consequences...are you telling me you are coming home to go up against me?"
"Wow Kay...I'm surprised at you. Are you saying you are participating in our destruction?"
Before I could respond to his baiting he continued...
"I would never go against you-you are my brother, but I am going at your kind."
"My kind...what kind is that?"
Resolutely J.B. looked me square in the eye.
"The chumps. Tell 'em Kay. Tell 'em Abandoned Nation, the real live wires, are coming."
Staring at a face I was born to love, I couldn't help thinking *my big bro done lost his mind.*
After the visit I sat in my apartment thinking about J.B.'s speech. I couldn't help marveling at his naivety. We both came to similar conclusions regarding the historical and modern conflict between our people and the powers that be. But our philosophies toward action differed tremendously.

While J.B. clearly wanted to follow the Malcolm X route, I felt differently. It wasn't just the speech; I was also tired of receiving his preachy type letters and the avoidance of politics in my response to his letters, seemed only to fuel his desire to set me straight.

I wrote him about taking papers, about building a team; I received prophecies of death and destruction in return. J.B. always underestimated my ability to think. To him, I was pure impulse and my actions would always be dictated by my urges. The more I thought about his speech, the greater my urge to respond. I decided to sit down and write him the most comprehensive letter I ever wrote in hopes that I might be able to reach him.

```
Dear J.B.;
     As always I reflect on your words and the
hopes that accompany them. I must say I truly
enjoyed your speech though I disagree with many
of your conclusions. Bro, you speak of the
struggle as if it's simply a matter of Black
and White. As if somehow the paper chase has
no part in the struggle. The paper chase...I
imagine this term makes you cringe because
somehow in your studies you've come to believe
that the only way to beat the system is from
within; like killing a spider while playing in
its web.
     Bro, my silence throughout these months
may have left you with the impression that your
advice has fallen on deaf ears, but it hasn't
and never will. When there's a break in my
hectic schedule, (always on the grind, please
don't cringe) I read the books you recommend.
     I agree that a war is being waged against
us. I agree that the disproportionate number of
Black and Latino folk in prison reflects the
nature of the war. I even agree that something
must be done. But what? I ponder the
solution, and my silence represents not my
indifference, but my appreciation for our
```

dilemma. J.B. you view the world through nostalgic eyes; though you study history you fail to truly grasp the lessons.

I hate to be the one to bust your bubble but the route of the Messiah type leader has proven foolish. As with Malcolm and countless others who seemingly died in vain to teach us, all men are vulnerable to the determination of the assassin. So in essence, the movement lasts only as long as the assassin or his controllers allow.

Fredrick Douglass argued that power concedes nothing without a demand. Protests and pickets, voting and praying only express our discomfort toward certain treatment. But you should know, that villains don't care about a victim's discomfort. His only concern is his safety and the booty. Thus, attacking the safety or the booty changes the rules of engagement immediately. Marcus Garvey once asked: "Black Man, where's your army?" My response is building a fuckin' team.

Our so-called leaders, (the ones you like to emulate) enjoy using popular slogans like: "No justice. No peace". Such tough words. And since our streets are peaceful (that is in our dealing with the government) I assume that the Tawanna Brawley, Eleanor Bumpus issues have been met with a just and fair result. What about Yusef Hawkins? Bro, it doesn't take a prophet to predict that many more violations and abuses against our people will occur.

History teaches that there are two universal languages-violence and Math. Remember it takes Math to build buildings and missiles. Violence and Math. Both are being used symbiotically against us. Until we learn, or choose to speak this language, no meaningful dialogue will ever materialize. Our discomfort is of little concern to our enemies. Moral reasoning and persuasive tactics don't work on a psychopath who historically has proven again and again to have absolutely no compassion or conscience in his pursuit of materials. Either we bust our guns or shut up. Great speeches are only boosts of vanity for the speaker. It makes you feel revolutionary but it doesn't make you one. If you are truly serious, then the team will be awaiting your arrival.

P.S. That live wire crap you were talking, leave that in Green Haven. When you give away your clothes and sneakers don't forget the rhetoric. It's nothing but a turn off in the real world.

Loyalty or DEATH
KK

A few days after the graduation I went to my mother's new apartment to help her put together her new wall unit and hang her curtains. 'Lil man was hanging out with me, a companionship I found intensifying daily. I was becoming attached to the little dude and looked forward to our time together. I wanted him to meet my mother, so that she could see for herself that everything Knee touched wasn't rotten.

My mother's door opened and to my surprise Alicia was standing there. She took one look at me, rolled her eyes and turned to walk away. I was so happy to see her that I smacked her on her ass and pulled her to me. She gave little resistance. I hugged her hard trying to let her feel how much I missed her. I whispered in her ear.

"*I'm sorry.*"

Her eyes quickly began watering as I parted her lips in search of forgiveness. She let me in. I was forgiven. Yeah, I apologized even though I hadn't a clue what I was apologizing for. I've learned that when it comes to women-every now and then it's good to say you're sorry. For them, sorry is the best word next to love - because both are words of surrender. 'Lil man began to giggle, perhaps he knew, even if I was still in denial. I was becoming a sucka vic for Alicia's love.

   *   *   *

CHAPTER 15
DECLARATION OF WAR

As was expected, in a matter of months under my management, our productivity increased and more importantly maintained its vitality. In other words, our three spots were booming and as far as the money went, things couldn't have looked better. At the end of each week, after all the workers were paid, the rents on our properties covered, Champ and I were stacking close to forty G's a piece. Compared to some operations we were considered small fries-but the race is not for the swift but for those that endureth. It was about longevity. Being able to make money for a very long time while avoiding detection is the face of success.

Those 100 Gs a week and better operations were impressive displays of suicidal hustling. I say suicidal because it was impossible for them to really think that they weren't under constant surveillance and investigation. That it wasn't just a matter of time before local or federal goons attacked. Though I mingled with these *ballers* I never once mentioned my observations about their flawed hustle. My reasoning was simple-their folly provided my team with adequate cover. While all eyes are on the peacocks no one pays attention to what's lurking in its shadow.

Out of the three spots we had, the one in L.E.S. was producing the least amount of currency but also the least amount of headaches. It was a smooth, predictable and discreet operation when compared to the Brooklyn and Queens spots. Though both these spots were considered gold mines there was always shit to be dealt with; from tension with rival teams, stick up kids with colorful names, sticky fingered workers and lieutenants who tried to add their own product to our reservoir unnoticed.

All these problems fell squarely on my shoulders, because Champ had proven a Chump when it came to administering discipline. In fact Champ's primary concern was collecting and spending his share. For him as quick at the profit came, it went. Between jewelry, cars and broads, Champ saw no other purpose. The ultimate peacock - my partner.

The jangle of a key chain worked like an alarm warning me of Alicia's presence at my front door. I was sitting on my couch, dressed in nothing but my silk Looney Tunes boxers watching the Cosby Show, when her excited voice threw me for a loop.

"Ooh Baby thank you so much, thank you soooo much!" Animated...Alicia was acting as though she'd won the lottery. Confused I stood up and stared, trying to figure out what was going on. Something was different about Alicia but I couldn't place it.

"Ooh Kameek, I opened it in front of my mother and she loves it more than me."

Bewildered, stalling for time, I asked...

"Your moms loves it?"

"Kameek, don't be silly. What woman wouldn't?"

Alicia extended her right arm as if handing a waiter her coat. It was this deliberate gesture that allowed me to finally identify the change. I could not believe my eyes. *Fuckin' bitch!* Battling for supremacy, all of my suppressed anger and hatred was turning my stomach in knots. With great difficulty I held my smile not wanting in anyway to worry Alicia or draw her any further into my darkness.

"Alicia...", my voice cracked with confusion. *"Alicia, I didn't...I didn't expect you to get it today."*

I lied and it hurt. What else could I do?

Dangling from Alicia's wrist was a multicolored unicorn bracelet. No need to examine its craftsmanship, I knew exactly what it was. The bracelet I stole and gave to Precious. Before I could craft the question, Alicia volunteered the answer.

"When I stopped by my mother's house today the package was already there."

"How...how long had it been there?"

"Well, mommy said it was there all week."

"Did you like the message?"

I asked hoping Precious left a clue to her intentions or whereabouts. Alicia's response confirmed my suspicions. Digging in her coat pocket she withdrew a note card and handed it to me.

The eggshell colored note card, held four words in a handwriting I knew all too well. *'We need to talk.'* The message, though brief, gave me my first sigh of relief. Precious, was sending me a message; looking for a truce while exposing my weakness. Pulling Alicia to me I hugged her, not wanting to lose her; but beginning to feel that it was time to let her go. My life was becoming riskier by the day. Each time I thought I covered a base another appeared exposed.

Tightly, I held Alicia, my nose buried in the fold of her neck savoring her fragrance. If I could've mustered enough courage, I would've called it quits-let the love of my life get on with her own. My hesitation solidified my cowardice. I knew I was being selfish, but like Samson I beheld my Delilah and felt my strength drain. I just couldn't wrap my tongue around the words of separation.

Then to make matters worse, the Brooklyn spot got robbed four times in one month. After each robbery I changed up the security and still the bandits got away, with the fourth robbery resulting in a shoot out in broad daylight between my team and the bandits. The result - a seven year old boy was shot in the shoulder and scored front-page stories in practically every newspaper in the city. Immediately the police shut the spot down for good. The incident began to plague my mind. How did these muthafuckas keep avoiding my traps? I kept coming up with the same conclusion. It had to be an inside job - but who?

I changed everything up from personnel to times and methods of delivery. I began to suspect that the police were behind it - perhaps the crooked cock suckas from the 75th or the 77th Precincts. This had to be the case because only an organized surveillance team could have picked apart my defense so effectively.

My suspicions grew ten fold when the spot in Queens took the same type of hit. It definitely was an inside job because the bastards were allowed into the spot by providing the daily password and color. I brought my suspicions to Champ thinking he may have an intelligent idea on how to proceed but in a nutshell his response was...

"*Kay...it comes with the territory.*"

Although what he said made sense that it all was a part of the game, I couldn't accept the feeling of going from looking for herbs to becoming one. The armor of a victim just didn't seem to fit comfortably.

And so once again I changed the security this time using a trick the Old God wrote about in a letter. Instead of just using codes and colors, I introduced hand signals. In addition to these new measures, without telling anyone I began doing my very own surveillance.

I paid a crack head named *Gail* to allow me to stay in one of her bedrooms. The windows of her apartment faced the building where my drugs were being sold. Gail had three small children and one teenage boy named *Junior*. He was around fourteen or fifteen and small for his age, but the hatred in his eyes whenever he looked at me, made up for his diminutive stature. I was an invader, and probably not the first to enter his sacred domain with the threat of disruption. But my concern was in the domain outside his window-caring very little about the lives on the inside. So shorty had nothing to worry about. With a cheap pair of binoculars I sat in that window and watched.

In the center of a poorly lit, dead end block, sat our crack den. Poorly lit, on account that once a week we paid a crack head to bust a few street lights; a poorly lit block makes surveillance just a tad bit more challenging.

Our spot sat invitingly on the second floor of a five story building. The building was divided into two sides, with five apartments on each floor, totaling fifty apartments for the entire building. Our money maker was on the left hand side or what the tenants called the *south side*. The inside of the building, though clean, had obviously witnessed better days. Both the landlord and superintendent were paid monthly for their continued silence.

In fact their uncanny ability to see no evil, hear no evil, frustrated the tenants and amused the police. Nevertheless, we were smart enough not to press our luck. Realizing that if the tenants got fed up enough they could collectively shut us down; we made sure that no crack head hung out or smoked inside or in front of the building.

The sidewalks were a totally different story. From Gail's fourth floor window I now possessed an aerial view of the crack jungle under my care. Despite the poor lighting, I was able to see the entire block with clarity.

Our spot was the only one on the block and so it was easy to keep track of the steady stream of fiends who came and went in their daily routine of chasing the dragon. The block had a number of abandoned parked cars which when the sun set, transformed into all purpose motel rooms-where the crack whores with their blistered lips turned their tricks. These motels had no use for electricity; the dim glow of the crack pipes provided the only light needed.

Though the beginning of Spring, the only three trees on the block were barren. Their leafless trunks ravaged by years of neglect and abuse. Their soil littered with crack vials, broken stems and empty beer cans. Such a normal sight that most people who lived on the block didn't even realize that the trees held no leaves and could provide no shade. Transfixed, I sat watching the madness. A superintendent patrolled the front of his building chasing fiends off with *Tiger,* his black and brown spotted pit bull.

Our clientele was a diversified lot; with every kind of character you could think of. From the suit and tie wearing businessman, to the Orthodox Jew wearing a beanie. From Chinese to Rasta our spot welcomed more nationalities than the United Nations. For me, the toughest sight to see was always the visibly pregnant women-bellies protruding with life, exiting my spot in full bliss-seemingly oblivious to their sacred calling. Champ's assessment of the moral dilemma came to mind...

"*Man Kay...if we don't sell it to them our competition will.*"

The auction of a brand new toaster went to the highest bidder; his bid-five dollars. While a gold chain with a big medallion hung from a fence on display-a freak's bizarre, whose proceeds belonged to me. A limo pulled up and a white guy with a fake mafia look, wearing a red and blue Fila suit stepped out of the sedan and ran inside the building. He emerged less than a minute later excited about his score.

A crack head named *Dino* tried to lure him into a conversation but the *made man* was no fool. I laughed to myself as he paid Dino no mind jumping back into the safety of the limo. Dino was a savvy fast talking fiend who could talk his way in or out of any situation. Yet, just as quickly as the limo came, it disappeared leaving Dino in the middle of the street scratching his head. Many of the crack whores were laughing hysterically taunting Dino for his failure.

My L.T. *Bop* pulled up as scheduled in his tan Cressida preparing to make his routine checkup. A long haired shorty sat comfortably in his passenger seat. Immediately all the crack heads, including Gail lined up in front of the building. I heard about this, but it would be my first time actually witnessing it. Bop stepped out of the car with his arms extended in the air. The fiends began clapping like groupies getting a glimpse of a movie star. Bop said something and they all, as if rehearsed, began laughing.

Bop reached into his pocket and pulled out an eight carat crack rock. Quickly he began crushing the rock into small pieces. Satisfied, he threw the crack high into the air allowing the chips to fall where they may. Without a second glance Bop entered the building and with equal disregard the crack heads paid his exit or Tiger's barking no mind.

On hand and knee, crack heads began searching the pavement, determined not to let even a crumb escape their inspection. The girl in Bop's car stuck her pretty head out of the window teasing the fiends by pointing to the ground and yelling over and over...

"*You missed a spot!*"

So powerful and debasing was Bop's gesture that when he returned ten minutes later, about half the original fiends and a handful of new ones were still on the ground separating natural pebbles from cocaine crumbs.

I grew so cold and callous in the pursuit of that scrilla that I didn't even see crack heads as actual people. To me they were-well crack heads. Zombie like creatures who couldn't be trusted, and Gail, who was still searching the pavement for a ticket to *Never Never Land*, was proving no different.

As the days went by I began to notice Gail's house hold routines. Junior would get up early in the morning and wake his siblings. They would then all get dressed quietly trying not to disturb their Mother's rest. Just as quietly, they would leave for school. They never ate breakfast and the more I thought about it, they didn't eat much at all.

One morning after the kids left, while Gail was still sleeping, I decided to look around the house. I was more than just being nosey-something in my gut kept telling me to explore. The entire crib was bare of any real appliances. The only TV and stereo was in the kids' bedroom. I quickly realized that Gail must have sold practically anything of value, yet refused, even under the hypnotic trance of King Crack to steal from her own children.

For the first time in my life I began imagining what it would've been like if my mother had fallen victim to crack when J.B. and I were young. The thought alone was suffocating and yet as much as I wanted to turn back and return to the empty room and my cheap binoculars, an inner tug kept pulling me toward the kitchen.

Upon entering the kitchen I immediately hit the light switch. Roaches scattered by the hundreds, unwashed plates in the sink while on the counter stood a clear open container of orange Kool Aid. Yeah...even after all these years, the details are still very vivid. After the roaches took cover, I approached the refrigerator and opened it.

Nothing! It might as well have been empty. A container of milk sat alone on a shelf while some left over Chinese food sat on another. That was it. For every conscience there is an awakening, a revelation, an experience or loss, which begins to force us to see things, by degrees, more clearly. Standing in front of that refrigerator staring for what must have been a good half hour at a vacant space, created the first doubt in my mind regarding the game I had grown to love.

     *   *   *

CHAPTER 16
REVELATIONS

Without a doubt I knew that the robberies were and inside job but couldn't figure out its source. Like a persistent fly it nagged at me. In Gail's crib for an entire week, I remained hidden truly believing that I would unravel the mystery. While I obviously hadn't come closer to finding any clues, I did discover that my gangsta armor had a chink.

Having been so consumed with the paper chase, I never before gave thought of the damage I was contributing to. Watching Gail and her children up close made the numbing of my conscience difficult. I couldn't help comparing Gail's household to the one J.B. and I grew up in. The only commonality was we both had absent fathers. Where my mother's home was full of life - plants, goldfish and laughter; Gail's gray dingy walls and reckless roaches were like an abusive relationship - it drained life. After sitting in that window for a clueless week I abandoned the mission. The day of my departure, I snatched Junior up and took him food shopping spending close to $700. Just watching shorty's expression as he tried to conceal his happiness was enough for me to momentarily justify my occupation.

Do you believe in destiny? I know. It's a strange question...but it's one that has plagued me throughout my life. I mean at times, life seems so spontaneous and unpredictable - random circumstances, but then there are times when it all seems scripted and we're nothing but actors following a script.

Such was the feeling I felt when Champ's Benz pulled up in front of the building that housed our crack spot. As he got out of the car he seemed really surprised to see a fellah.

"Kay...where the hell you been at? I started getting worried partner."

Champ sounded more concerned than his body language let on. Yet for some reason I paused in my response and gave him a long penetrating look. I learned that when looking in a person's eyes, as if you already know what they are hiding,

there's a strong probability that you may rattle them into exposing their hand. Yeah I was bluffing. It felt like I was following a script I had no control over. His response was totally unexpected.
> "*Fuck you staring at me like I robbed the spots or something.*"

I was caught off guard with that one. Of course it was Champ-it all added up. Aside from myself, he was the only other person with unhindered access to all the spots and since I know I didn't rob myself Champ's guilt became unquestionable. My response was immediately icy.
> "*If I felt that way I'd kill you on the spot.*"

He grinned and so did I. I continued...
> "*Actually, I've been staking this spot out hoping these clowns strike again.*"
> "*How long you been here?*"
> "*About a week.*"

We were walking toward the spot - two gladiators keeping our eyes trained on each other. I felt the tension and knew that the unsaid declaration of war had been initiated. Ice water expanded in my veins with each step I took.
> "*Kay I keep telling you that it's all a part of the game-it comes with the territory.*"

He held the hallway door open for me searching for signs of my mistrust.
> "*Yeah...but I keep telling you I ain't playin' no games*",

I shot back.
I walked through the door nonchalantly giving him my back.
> "*You can't stress yourself over this shit.*"

Our spot was on the second floor and so we both took the stairs. I was in the lead taking two steps at a time. Champ was right behind me still talking reckless. But all I could hear was the Old God's question playing in my mind...
> '*What do you know about the nature of a man, especially around large quantities of money? It's one thing to know a person when ya both broke and hungry. What happens when the belly starts to fill and the hamburger is no longer big enough to share? When the stage is*

Honor Amongst Thieves

only big enough for one star? Can you detect smokeless fire son? Can you?'

Champ's annoying voice broke the memory...

"Eventually them niggas will slip up, mark my words."

And with that final insult Champ sealed his fate. Having reached the top of the second floor landing, I spun around to face him-gun already in my palm. Champ was still climbing the stairs when my sudden movement triggered his boxing instincts. Reflexively he squared into a defensive position, perhaps prepared to defend against a punch or a kick but his eyes verified my hidden suspicions about all them boxing niggas-that their profession taught no counter punch for a well placed bullet, especially five from a .44 Bulldog.

Killing a snake should never be a course of regret. I mean think about it-their very nature means that eventually they will bite. In an era where bosses are telling on their underlings and entire crews are playing the *last one is the rotten egg* games when the FEDS begin to snatch them up; there can be no room for benefits of doubt. You slip, you pay-it's that simple. I thought about Divine and Rick's suspicions and knew that I made the right move. Champ's death was the consequence of his own actions, not mine. There was only one problem with this entire scenario. The clown didn't die!

"UN - FUCKIN' BELIEVABLE!!!",

I yelled staring at myself in my bathroom mirror. It was five days since the shooting. Since I stood over his lifeless body and dumped two more shots in him just to be on the safe side. Yet, the phone call I just received made my stomach queasy. Would he tell the police or would he keep it in the streets? The most dreaded part of playing the game of chess is anticipating the opponent's next move. I had no choice. The ball was squarely in his court. Either way it was war. Having seen first hand what being buried alive meant I refused to return to prison at any cost. The police would get their pay's worth if they came fuckin' with me as well as anybody else who decided to side with the snake. Alicia's voice coming from the bedroom broke my train of thought but not before I once again found myself ready for war. Little did I know *Innocence* would be the ultimate casualty.

CHAPTER 17
WAR FRONT

The spots were mine. Two months since the shooting and my ears on the streets told me Champ was recuperating somewhere in Delaware. He was wheel chair bound and thus greatly hindered in his ambitions. My ears told me that he reached out to a couple of live wires apprising them of his version-a move that showed how desperate he was for some help. As for me, it was business as usual. However, instead of splitting the pot of gold two ways it was now all mine.

Naturally, I knew enough to move a lot more cautiously. Sometimes I went days on end without showing my face and when I did appear, it would be a brief cameo appearance before fading off again. I also hired some shooters, putting them on standby. Since the day I left prison I was slowly building an impressive arsenal. My man Ice-the one who saved my neck in the mess hall riot-came home and I immediately made him my right hand man. Allowing Ice to run the day-to-day operations gave me the time to figure out how to clean up all the money I was stacking.

There were a couple of businesses that caught my interest. However, my uncle finally convinced me to invest in his dream of opening a *Radio Shack*. At first I thought he was buggin' but the more I studied its market, the more I realized that technology was the course of the future and so on April 23, 1990, approximately eighteen months after my release, I held my grand opening ceremony as a silent partner with my uncle and the regional representatives of the Radio Shack franchise. Our store was located right off the main artery leading to and from Jamaica Estates where the rich Black folks lived. Every penny for the endeavor came from me-yet the business was in my uncle's name only. While I had no worries about him robbing me, the feeling of one day being able to have something legit in my own name nagged at me.

Both my mother and Alicia attended the opening. My moms volunteered to *man the counter* for the first six months to help us save money and get the business off the ground. By all predictions, this would be a slow but profitable grind. I took over fifty pictures and sent them to J.B., Knee, Sha and the Old God determined to show them the fruits of my labor. I caught the entrepreneurial bug and immediately began looking for other investments.

Behind the shooting my name was once again ringing bells in the streets. If you've been paying attention to my story you know at one time I would have loved the spotlight. But now such attention could only serve as a hindrance. I worked so hard to stay below radar yet once again I was in the eye of the storm. Many dudes want their names to be spoken of in the streets-you know that peacock mentality, never realizing the primary source of info for the police is in the street chatter. The more your name is spoken the greater the possibility to get caught up in an investigation. It was in the midst of all this I decided it was a good idea to become invisible for a while. It was time to take my first vacation and give the hood a rest. Ice was doing such a good job I had no doubts about leaving the fort in his hands.

Besides, I was wrestling with another dilemma that needed to be settled. Alicia was causing me more stress than I could continue to allow. I needed to know exactly where she stood. She had been living with me in my Sheepshead Bay condo for the past three months, slowly turning my crib into a feminine abode. Four foot smiling teddy bears lined my bedroom wall like out of shape soldiers guarding their lioness. An entire closet full of Alicia's clothes appeared out of nowhere, leopard spotted panties swinging from a line in the bathroom, while other items made just for women were staking their claim on the shelves above my toilet.

Like a thief in the night Alicia's home invasion was being executed with near perfect stealth. These were all signs she wanted more out of our relationship. Yet I couldn't help feeling as though we were walking on eggshells around one another. It was as if we were both scared to disrupt the delicate balance of peace and love with talks of the future. Coming home to her smile every night felt right, living with her the past few months only served to reinforce my love for her. Unabashed smiles would appear on my face whenever I thought of her for long; add to this, the extra heart beats that seized control of my heart whenever I was in her presence and the recipe for disaster was present. Yeah, some real sucka vic for love shit was brewing inside of me and therein laid the problem. If my feelings weren't placed in the proper perspective-Alicia would become my *Achilles Heel*. My uncertainty about our future would become a distraction that could prove costly. I needed to find out what was really on her mind and in her heart. Either way I told myself I had to be prepared for a future with or without her.

Alicia was on Spring Break and so we booked a flight to the Bahamas. With Alicia's urging I left my sky pager back at the apartment and was committed to just enjoy life. Our departure from Kennedy was met with beautiful clear skies. My first time ever flying on a plane and like a kid in an amusement park, I felt giddy. Alicia was excited as well but for an entirely different reason. She had always wanted to go to the Bahamas and the trip for her, was a dream come true. She flew many times with her parents, visiting relatives in Chicago, Denver and San Diego. So when the turbulence hit and the plane began jumping up and down, before my calm and cool composure could really be put to the test, Alicia calmly explained what was happening and why. That was one of the qualities I loved about her-her uncanny ability to calm the savage beast. She knew when to say what needed to be said or do what needed to be done. I once teased her by saying she would make a hell of a gangsta if she had only been born a man.

The funny thing was Alicia didn't take it as a compliment, in fact she took it as an insult. She was cool with the gangsta part; it was the *if only she had been born a man* part that rattled her. Alicia is of the mind set that anything a man can do a woman can do just as well if not better, including being a gangsta. She even taught me something I never would have believed possible if she hadn't proven it five different ways.

Through her college studies, Alicia discovered in ancient times there were no such things as male gods. All the deities were feminine in nature. Thus the oldest concept of God was of a Mother. At first I found the concept that mankind once worshipped a Cosmic Mother and not Father, strange and uncomfortable. But the more I thought about it, the more it all made sense. If truth were told, man still views women as Gods. Practically everything we do is for their attention and adoration. Even in the hood, most crimes committed have at its roots-a woman. Think about it. Dudes sell drugs to acquire money in order to buy clothes, cars, jewels and homes-all in an effort to become more appealing to the woman of their dreams.

I even thought about my mother and how I always viewed her without giving her the name-my God. As a child when I used to come home from school with good grades on a test, the thoughts of Jesus, Buddha or Allah being proud of me never entered my mind. My only concern was showing the result to my mother. It was her praise that magnified my accomplishments and made me feel like doing it again. When I did wrong I wasn't afraid of the wrath of an unseen god in the sky-I was afraid of the one in my house whose wrath was sometimes nothing more than a disappointed stare. So I began to see where Alicia was coming from. She was able to make me aware of how chauvinistic I sounded in many conversations. How indoctrinated I became to the notion that women couldn't function without men. In the hood we are taught in words and deeds, that women are like crippled mutes without us. Just a piece of pussy is what the streets whispered into the ears of young men. I felt fortunate to have in my corner a woman who wasn't just a piece of ass, who wasn't afraid to challenge and bring out the best in me. I mean, isn't that what all men truly desire-a true connection with God? When I was in Alicia's presence I knew I discovered heaven.

As the plane descended, the Caribbean heat engulfed us and we knew we were on Bahamian soil. I always thought summers in N.Y.C. were hot but this took the cake. As we walked through the airport I couldn't help noticing all the Black faces; the police and all the other important looking people were of African stock. I took it all in delicately, as if I was sipping a hot cup of cocoa in the dead of winter - every sip savored. An overwhelming sense of belonging came over me and for the first time in a long time, longer than I could recall, I was at peace.

Back at the travel agency I decided to rent a limo - I wanted to feel for once like a visiting dignitary. Our limo driver turned out to be a guy named *Carl*. Tall and extremely thin, so thin that at first glance the word *anorexic* came to mind. Bald headed with a nose like an eagle he sported a sharp goatee and dark shades. As soon as he heard Alicia speak he dropped his Bahamian accent and began speaking in a N.Y. dialect.

"*Let me guess...you guys are from N.Y.C.*"

"*Yeah...Brooklyn,*" Alicia responded.

"*Small world,*" Carl muttered to himself loud enough for us to hear.

"*I grew up in Crown Heights-right off of Dean and Bedford*"

He said in a matter of fact tone.

"*Small world,*" I agreed.

"*So I guess you got tired of living in the chaos?*" Alicia nosily inquired.

> "*Yeah you can say that, I mean don't get me wrong, I love the city. You know, it's blend of cultures, the nightlife and so on. But the fast pace...it is just too crazy.*"

I began to tune Carl out. I was too busy hanging my head out of the window taking in all of the sights and sounds. So many bright colors and smiling faces, this was truly a foreign land. It dawned on me that there were twice as many trees, flowers and grass than buildings and concrete; another reality beyond my experience.

Slowly the limo came to a halt. In front of us, a crowd of children in uniforms held hands while crossing the street. The innocence in their laughter sent chills down my spine - *what the hell was coming over me?* Carl's voice came back into focus.

> "*It's so hard to find yourself, in a place so overcrowded and congested with so many distractions. See, down here, life is taken in stride-there's no rush.*"

We were moving once more, the cacophony of the children's laughter fading by the second.

> "*I mean...don't get me wrong-paradise is only for you tourists. Us natives have our share of problems, times*

*are hard for many. We even have crack heads poppin'
up right to left..."*
Damn! Like Napoleon, King Crack was attempting to conquer
the world!
*"...the crazy thing is the authorities have no idea how
serious this problem can get."*
"Yeah it can get pretty ugly," I quickly added.
I wanted to change the depressing mood that Carl's convo was
beginning to cause.
*"So Carl...outside of all the places this wonderful
brochure mentions, are there any other places we need
to check out?"*
Carl's smile said it all.
"Bredren...I thought you'd never ask."
Carl dropped us off in front of our hotel and handed us his
business card.

Our suite was spacious yet cozy. I immediately walked to the terrace and stood in awe. Below me was the resort's Olympic size swimming pool, while directly in front of me stood an unfamiliar Atlantic; far different from the polluted one I was used to seeing in N.Y. This Atlantic was calm and green with an occasional march of snow capped waves that seemed to stare back at me. For as far as the eye could see, water and birds ruled the landscape.

Alicia slid into my arms and we both just stood there for what felt like an eternity staring at the dusky indigo horizon; transfixed by the sun's slow dive into the ocean and the blend of colorful vapors that surrounded the sacred union of fire and water. It was mesmerizing, picturesque; a scene born for a postcard.

Al Greene once sang that you can't color a thought or touch an emotion - meaning that there are some events or moments in our lives that defy description-this was such a moment. Finally the sun disappeared into the ocean's womb and I carried Alicia into the master bedroom.

With our luggage still unpacked, I slowly stripped Alicia naked. Her body, as beautiful as the Caribbean itself, stood before me, mine to possess. Slowly Alicia stripped me, all the while staring at me as if seeing me for the very first time. We kissed. Gently, I laid Alicia on the king sized bed, glistening like a diamond her skin deflected the soft rays of the Caribbean sunset. Her skin, her eyes, lips and body was perfect. She was perfect. She made me whole. As I kissed her lips my hands fondled her breast making her nipples firm under the pressure. I placed her breast in my mouth sucking and nibbling on her nickel sized nipples, while my fingers found their way towards her wet spot.

She opened up and guided my fingers inside. I felt her muscles tighten as I played inside of her; my thumb rubbing against her clit, causing her juices to run freely down my fingers. I pulled them out and hungrily placed them in my mouth, licking each finger, tasting her, wanting more. Damn she tasted so good. I pulled her to the edge of the bed and got on my knees. I began sucking on her clit while my fingers went in and out of her pussy. She was moving her hips uncontrollably and I felt the blood rushing to my dick. As I took my fingers out and plunged my tongue inside her, she grabbed my head pushing my face and tongue deeper. After a few minutes of tasting her, I knew I had to be in her.

Licking her belly, I made my way to her breast and then her lips. While we kissed, her hands gently began coaxing and massaging my dick. She stroked it - long and slow. Rubbing the head of my dick against her wet pussy, she gently guided me inside her. I could feel her muscles contracting every time I rocked in and out.

Arching her back and lifting her hips, allowed me to squeeze deeper and deeper inside. Her breathing grew heavy, her moaning and panting more frequent. Like a raging bull I built momentum - the pain from her scratching my back blissful, her way of marking her territory. Thrust after thrust, grind after grind, behind each stroke I placed my entire being - until she exploded.

Alicia began bucking, her pussy muscles contracting on its own, her words no longer obscene - she spoke in tongue. A chain reaction defeated my control and I found myself spewing my life force deep into her womb, as I felt her heartbeat slow down to a steady rhythm while her body remained entwined with mine, I knew that this was heaven. I closed my eyes and prayed, *"Please don't let me lose her."*

Tightly, as if my life itself depended on it, I hugged her, all the while planting kiss after kiss all over her neck and face until nature caught up to us and round two began. Spreading her legs true and wide once more I penetrated her slowly. Not as slow as the sun entering the womb of the ocean but with the same artistic attempt-the sacred union of fire and water was once more recreated. Alicia and I made love the entire night as if it were our first and last time together.

The following days went by like a blur. We enjoyed the sights and sounds as we island hopped our way throughout the Bahamas. It was there that I first fell deeply in love with *Conch*, a native shellfish of the Bahamas. Our days were spent mostly in the water or by it. We went wind sailing, snorkeling, jet skiing and canoeing. We were given a tour of the fabled underwater lost city. We saw with our own eyes the *Bimini Road*, huge pillow shaped blocks stretched out on the hallow sea floor, clearly resembling a paved road, whose secrets seemed heavily guarded by occasional schools of nurse sharks. Alicia and I slept nude on white sand, another Hallmark moment.

Like Adam and Eve, we found paradise enchanting. Our nights were spent in this order - gambling, dancing and fuckin'. Only our first night was set aside for lovemaking. After that we loved making each other's freak come out. Despite having the time of my life I kept resisting the urge to call Ice and see how the spots were holding up. In the end I was committed to having a good time and so I didn't give into the persistent whisper. Alicia and I were waist deep in the emerald green sea giggling and laughing when I turned serious.

"Baby...we need to talk."
"About what?"
"About us...about the future."
Alicia's face darkened, her eyebrows squinted with suspicion.
"What about us?"
"Where do we go from here? We've been together four years and I've grown to love you. I love you! Not just

your pretty eyes, or stripper body, not just your wonderful cooking or that sexy way you bite your lip when you study for tests. I love you-your heart, your ambitions, everything that is Alicia-I love. But Baby...I'm in these streets hard. I won't stand here and tell you no sucka shit like there ain't no jobs for me, because the truth is I never even bothered to look for one. I have absolutely no desire to bust my ass for someone else, no desire to live in the margins of society. It's all or nothing for me Baby. It's all or nothing. The more money I make the more I will invest in opening up legitimate businesses, until I'm able to walk away on top. That's my plan. But there's no timetable, there's no guarantee that I will make it to the finish line alive. It's a dirty game and I have no illusions about my chances for success. If I stay focused I have a chance, if I lose focus I'm finished. This is why I gotta know where you stand because my uncertainty about us is becoming a distraction..."

Alicia had heard enough. She put her finger to my lips and interrupted.

"*Kameek...ever since I could remember I always wanted to be a doctor...*"

I interrupted.

"*Even if we break up I'll still foot the bill for you...*"

Once again Alicia put her finger to my lips then continued.

"*As I got older becoming a doctor seemed unreachable...not just financially but spiritually as well. Kameek, I no longer believed in myself. I no longer believed in my potential and so I buried the dream, but you believed in my dream and you made me believe in it again. You gave me my wings. I've thought long and hard about us. I even spoke to your mother and mine both of them telling me I can do better, but better than what? Who could make me happier than the man who resurrected my dreams? When I'm with you I am alive-I feel safe. When I am not with you I merely exist - you are my other half. I do not agree with your lifestyle but no matter what happens, however this goes down, I'm with you until the sun burns out!"*

"Until the sun burns out?"

"UNTIL THE SUN BURNS OUT!"

She was poking my chest with her finger to make sure I got the message. I smiled needing to hear those exact words. We began play fighting in the water again, when a speedboat sped by and an orange bag fell off the boat and into the water about fifty feet away from us.

The owner of the boat, oblivious to his lost property, sped out of sight as Alicia and I swam into the deep water to retrieve it. Imagining it being a couple of kilos of coke I swam with vigor. I snatched the bag. It was extremely light. *So much for the keys of coke theory.* We brought the bag back to shore expecting it to have a name on it or something. But the only writing was the word *DESTINY* printed on the lapel of the bag.

By this time curiosity had the best of both of us so we opened the bag. It was full of gold gift wrapping paper. As we began emptying the paper onto the sand, a tiny black velour box with a gold ribbon appeared. It seemed that the paper was only used to protect this box. The mystery deepened and both of us were salivating to discover its secrets. Written on the ribbon of the box was again the word *DESTINY.* Slowly I lifted the cover and the glow from a huge clear diamond rock deflected the sun's rays into a prism of a million different hues; the rock itself was attached to a pink and gold ring. Just as the realization of it all began to sink in on Alicia I was down on one knee...

"Alicia will you marry me?"

She screamed in excitement and began punching me in the shoulder. Her punches began to sting so I stood up. She covered her face with her hands. I drew her to me and she wrapped her arms tightly around my waist. Raindrops began falling from her eyes-she was crying.

"I thought you would never ask...I thought you would never ask..."

For two long weeks Alicia and I played husband and wife in paradise. Our very own *Fantasy Island* minus Mr. Roark and that little nigga Tattoo. When I think back to that vacation it wasn't the snorkeling, wind sailing or the unhindered sex that sticks out. It was the laughter. Free from the stress and strains of life in the Big Apple, we were able to reaffirm our love for each other. God, did I love this woman, and paradise allowed me to show her how much. We found humor in everything from the cab driver with the fake accent who got lost driving us from one resort to a private air field or the helicopter ride from the Bahamas to Miami to attend Alicia's sorority party.

But paradise never lasts forever. We arrived back at Kennedy on a rainy May morning. The dreary weather felt like a bad omen. While still in the airport I called my mother to make sure she was OK. Hearing her voice calmed my nerves and after promising to tell her all about my trip when I got home, I hung up.

As soon as we reached our apartment I looked at my sky pager and saw that Ice's emergency code filled up the screen. *So much for paradise.* After about four calls I finally tracked Ice down. He was glad to hear my voice and wasted no time getting to the point.

"*Yo…I had to let these sucka muthafuckas feel it.*"
"*Who?*"
"*Papa Doc and them clowns.*"
Ice's voice grew more excited by the second.
"*What? What happened?*"
"*Man…don't you read the papers?*"
"*I was in the Bahamas or did you forget?*"
I was growing annoyed. Ice continued…
"*Anyway…about two days after you left, that clown Richie Rich shows up in front of the spot asking for you.*"
"*Yeah so…*"
"*So I'm thinkin' nuffin' of it. I ask him do he want your beeper number. He said nah, just tell you he stopped by. He jumped in the Pathfinder and took off. Next day he shows up again, this time he's talkin' real aggressive tellin' me your days are numbered and that Papa Doc bought the spot from Champ.*"
"*Really?*"

> "Yeah man...that nigga actually asked me did I want a job and how much was the spot makin'."
>
> "What you say?"
>
> "I told him I had to think about it. He gave me his beeper number and told me to beep him when you came around. But he didn't want me to tell you about the beep-he was tryin' to get me to set you up."

I was silent.

Papa Doc was an impressive figure. Having his hands in everything from extortion and racketeering to drugs and prostitution. He's what we called a diversified crook. His biggest claim to fame was in providing the muscle for a move made against John Gotti's sanitation monopoly in Brooklyn. The major fallacy being when Gotti was on top, nothing happened without his blessing. The truth is NYC is too big and too gritty for one man to ever claim and while Gotti was the poster child for gangstas-a real live White peacock; there were many other gangstas of darker complexions who had no qualms about stepping on the Dapper Don's feet. Papa Doc was by all accounts a man of this caliber.

Truthfully, my initial reaction was to accept the loss. In fact that was the wise and prudent move to make and I was, just this once, prepared to bow out gracefully, but then Ice dropped the bombshell. Interpreting my silence as permission to continue...

> "So I loaded up the team."
>
> "What team?"

My anxiety began to build.

> "My team...a few little shooters I got from out of the East. Anyway...I beeped the clown boy Rich and told him you was on your way."
>
> "Ah man Ice...what did you do?"
>
> "Fuck you mean 'what did I do'? They came to kill you! They pulled up seven cars deep with the Big Kahuna himself in the last car."

My blood was boiling and I wasn't sure if it was because of Ice's gung-ho mentality or Papa Doc's arrogant assumption that I would go out without a fight. Ice continued.

"*Fuck I supposed to do? We caught them clowns sleeping and let 'em have it.*"
"*Who...Papa Doc?*"
"*Nah. We missed that old muthafucka. He literally had niggas jumpin' in front of bullets for him and shit.*"
"*So some of 'em got hit?*"
"*Yeah man. It was all in the papers and everything. We hit four of 'em and laid that clown boy out.*"
"*Who...Rich?*"
"*Yeah. Rich.*"
"*Get the fuck outta here?*"
"*Nah Kay. I can't make no shit like this up. The spots are lost. Homicide is all over the one in Corona and Papa Doc took over the one in the L.E.S.*"

All I could do was close my eyes wishing I could've stayed with Alicia in paradise forever but the real world with real nightmares was once again my lot in life.

After arranging a time to meet with Ice; I hung up the phone and just sat there thinking long and hard on how to handle this. With shots fired-blood spilled and Papa Doc's left hand man dead; there could be no other option but war. I thought about the move Champ made and truly admired his cunning. Wheelchair bound, probably broke financially from his flamboyant lifestyle; going up against me would prove foolish. By selling the spots to Papa Doc, he smoothly placed me and the O.G. in each other's cross hairs.

What puzzled me was this: with all Doc had going for him, why would he take on a confrontation for chump change? Going to war with me for such a small operation didn't seem well thought out; a bit impulsive in fact. Champ must have fed him a bunch of bullshit-from the spots clearing close to 100 Gs a day to my reputation being nothing but a good P.R. campaign. Two thoughts entered my mind. The first was Champ's plan might actually backfire. The other was Doc's impulsiveness may prove flawed and easily exploitable.

I went to the newsstand by the train station and found three days worth of articles pertaining to the shoot out. Not much information was given the first two days other than it being the result of *an apparent drug feud between two rival posses*. They also had a picture of Richard "*Richie Rich* " Smith right next to his rap sheet. Rich was from the south side of Queens, who despite his criminal past overcame the challenges to become a productive member of his community. *A bunch of bullshit.*

After reading the first two days worth of papers I suspected that either the police knew very little or everything- and were simply holding their cards close to their chests. The third day's worth of information proved me right. By the third day, the shoot out was considered prehistoric and thus subjected to a small article on the fifth page of Newsday and the seventh page of The Post. Both articles were chillingly identical in nature; a clear sign that both were fed by the same source; the police.

The article was titled, "The Ice Man's Deadly Agenda", in The Post and "The Ice Man's Takeover", in Newsday. The articles claimed that a mysterious gangsta known only by his nickname *Ice Man* was believed, by the cops to be responsible for the death of Rich, a number of other murders and shootings including Champ's. This string of violence was described as Ice's attempt to corner the drug trade in Corona.

With each passing minute my nightmare darkened. The police were clearly fishing for information trying to figure out who Ice was and then the man behind the monster. I also understood that the game changed considerably in the last five years. The tremendous amounts of money made in the crack game proved the death nail for the code of the street. Immediately a verse from the O.G. Bible came to mind:

LIKE THE GODS OF THE EGYPTIANS,
THERE ONCE EXISTED IN OUR HOODS MANY RULES AND TABOOS,
YET THE REIGN OF KING CRACK USHERED IN A NEW WAY OF LIFE,
A NEW LAW.
THE LAW OF ANY THING GOES.
WHAT WAS ONCE SHUNNED AND FROWNED UPON IS NOW GLORIFIED.

SNITCHES HAVE BECOME CELEBRITIES ABLE TO WALK THE STREET WITHOUT
FEAR OF REPRISALS.
ANYTHING GOES-THE NEW CREED OF THE JUNGLE.
*   *   *

With this spiritual jewel firmly in mind I knew that I had to proceed with caution. One wrong move, one stone left unturned and my life would be reduced to just another sad statistic; either six feet under or the rest of my days in a lonely cell. Both choices were unappealing. I was determined to come out of this on top; a decisive decision, a mounting confidence the police and Papa Doc would not overcome.

All successful Generals must approach war with a cautious yet inventive eye. Your strategy must have a basis in reality while your reality is shaped by sound information. This is a crucial point, far overlooked in the concrete jungles. All militaries rely on information or what they call *logistics* to help them determine the best course to take. In fact a large part of any army's budget is spent on gathering data or what they call reconnaissance missions. The Art of War, an ancient Chinese book on war principles dedicates an entire chapter, "*The Use of Spies*", and at least fifty other paragraphs to the importance of obtaining accurate information. In the O.G. Bible the stress on the importance of understanding the SCIENCE OF WAR is always present. That is because war is a science and like any physician who studies the symptoms of a disease to determine the cause and cure; a worthy General approaches the theater of war with the same reverence and respect.

Papa Doc was vulnerable in a number of ways. He had a few legit operations that could be shut down without any real difficulty. There were a few peacocks that were secretly on Doc's payroll. They played the part of being the man but I knew what they were-puppets and Doc their puppeteer. I also understood that in a prolonged war the advantage went to him. It wasn't about winning battles as much as it was about winning the war.

Ice wanted us to take back the L.E.S. spot and let that be where the *shit pops off*. I was saddened by his choice because he revealed so many flaws in his thinking. I knew the stars and stripes of a General would always escape him.

"Listen Ice..."

We were sitting in the living room of my apartment in Sheepshead Bay.

"...this ain't no game. This is war. People die. This nigga Papa Doc's arms are so long that for every soldier we could put in the field he could place ten."

Ice was shaking his head not believing what he was hearing. I continued.

"His money is so long that he could pay our own people to turn on us."

Ice interrupted.

"Kay...what's happening to you? All this money is makin' you soft."

He was looking at me as if I just told him I was extremely ill. I never had patience for idiots and my fuse was burning short. I ignored his comment and continued.

"It's not about going soft. It's not about puttin' up a good fight..."

I pointed to my head.

"...it's about winning the fuckin' war."

The look on Ice's face told me that he still wasn't convinced but at least he was paying attention.

"We're gonna lay low and let the information pour in. I'm waiting on a couple pieces of info. One piece in *particular and then I'm gonna show you what this shit is really all about."*

While waiting for that key piece of information to surface I decided to unleash my goons. I could sense their restlessness and knew they needed a mission. Though I was reluctant to engage Papa Doc in an all out war I understood the need to keep the sucka on the defensive.

Papa Doc, had a number of legitimate businesses. In Brooklyn he owned a string of butcher shops and a bakery. I knew their locations and kept eyes on all of them. His two auto shops in the Bronx were nothing more than junkyards. So I left behind no surveillance. I was unable to find out what operations he had going on in Manhattan and Staten Island but I knew something existed; I just couldn't place a finger on what. I decided to focus on his sanitation company. He co - owned a private sanitation company called *Doctor's Dirt*. His six sanitation trucks serviced some of the most wealthy and affluent neighborhoods in Queens and Long Island. I ordered my goons to put a stop to *Doctor's Dirt* house calls.

By no means did I expect my actions to cripple Doc. That wasn't my plan. My purpose was to frustrate him with distractions the way a fly would an elephant. I needed time to gather the necessary information and build up my war machine, while keeping him from mounting his own offensive.

I received an interesting phone call from Dice, the day after I shut the sanitation operation down. After a few minutes of small talk Dice finally got to the point. I imagined Sam being somewhere in the background.

"*Young Blood...* "

A name he began calling me in order to demonstrate his perceived rank,

"*...you know war is bad for business?*"

"*Yeah I know but it seems my hands are tied. Ice dusted off one of Doc's top lieutenants. You know the rule: when blood's shed beef can never be dead.*"

"*Well Kay, that's not necessarily always the case...think about it. Above all else, like you, Doc is a businessman. Would you agree?* "

"Definitely."

"And since war is bad for business then it's not necessarily what Doc wants- would you agree?"

"I'm following you."

"So the key is to find a way for Doc to save face."

"Save face? Man that nigga should've never stuck his face in my business to begin with."

Dice sighed that Father knows best sigh and quickly changed tactics.

"So this lieutenant of yours, Ice is his name right?"

"Yeah..."

Sadly, I could see where his train of thought was leading.

"Kay, problems will always arise when soldiers do what they want
and not what they are told. It's obvious that he wasn't acting on your orders because you were in the Bahamas when the shit went down."

Dice was playing a deadly game. He was trying to convince me to separate myself from Ice. Then what? Betray him to the wolves? Before Dice went any further I decided to nip his line of reasoning in the bud.

"Actually, Ice was following my direct orders-from the Bahamas. Being a lieutenant means defending the base."

"Yeah but Kay..."

"Ain't no buts, that's my man, my team, my call"

I was getting hyped.

"I thought you was calling me about business."

"We are talking business."

"Yeah, my business as opposed to our business."

"Kay, if you go to war it becomes my business."

He had a point there so I remained silent.

"Kay, all I'm saying is if you can avoid an all out war- it's wise to do so."

"By selling out my man?"

"Look I apologize if it sounded like I was suggesting you give Ice up. You know full well I respect your loyalty; though your sense of loyalty differs a little from mine."

"*Yeah, it's a tradition rather unique to Brooklyn*", I shot back.

Dice erupted in laughter momentarily breaking the tension.

"*I guess I deserved that one as well. But seriously Kay, and I'm gonna leave you with this thought-if you can squash this without anymore bloodshed-please pursue the course.*"

"*Dice, I respect what you're kicking, but dukes, it's not my call.*"

"*Kay, you're attacking his legitimate operations. That's hitting below the belt. You're provoking a response from him.*"

How did Dice know I was attacking Doc's businesses?

"*Nah, that's called reminding him of his vulnerabilities. Perhaps, if he sees that I'm willing to hit him where it hurts he just might discover he's lost the appetite for war.*"

"*OK, but what if that don't work?*"

"*Then I annihilate him!*"

"*You sound confident about this.*"

"*Well I don't intend to loose if that's what you mean.*"

"*Sometimes Kay, we can end up loosing even when we are victorious.*"

"*Sounds too philosophical for me; I'll just stick to the basics. Here's the bottom line Dice, I'm not budging. Either he backs down or we fill the fuckin' arena for the main event.*"

Thus my conversation with Dice. He left me with a lot to think about, a whole lot. I kept playing our conversation over and over in my head. *Words are key.* An alarming thought kept teasing my conscious but every time I attempted to corner the thought it fled. Two nights later, I awoke in the middle of the night with what to me felt like an epiphany.

Since the very beginning Papa Doc's actions made no sense. There was no rhyme or reason. Why would a man of Doc's stature allow himself to be suckered into a turf war? It was this part of the puzzle where the pieces just didn't fit. Unless...Doc's move was influenced by something or someone bigger than Champ. I sat on the edge of my bed disgusted with myself for not seeing it sooner. Dice, or his so - called circle of friends could pull something like this off. I thought back to the meeting with Dice in Sylvia's. Even back then he was looking for a way to tap into Brooklyn. What I couldn't figure out was the exact game plan-but I knew with a certainty that Dice was the unseen hand in this.

Either he was trying to push Doc and me into a messy war, where after the authorities cleaned up the mess, Dice would be in a position to set up shop and fill the void. Or he was somehow connected to Doc and felt it was time to move me out of the picture. But why? I just couldn't see the angle.

I decided to share my thoughts with someone whose opinion I respected. I drove to Handbone's crib. He lived in a one bedroom apartment in the Red Hook section of Brooklyn. It was a handsome apartment, fully furnished. His living room reflected his personality-carefully deliberate. There was his black leather and deep mahogany living room set. A school of colorful fish swam carefree in a 100-gallon fish tank that sat against the wall. Hanging directly above the tank were two sterling silver Samari swords with Japanese carvings engraved on its handles. No television anywhere in sight, instead a massive bookshelf replete with books sat on the opposite wall; obviously a lover of books-and fish.

I began laying my thoughts out to Handbone, hoping that I was just being paranoid. But Handbone, after hearing me out supported my suspicions.

"*The only thing that doesn't make sense to me is the angle.*"

"*What ya mean?*" he asked.

"*I mean the motive, what's his plan?*"

"*Well...*"

Handbone began then paused for an eternity, considering his words carefully,

"*...the first clue was when he suggested you abandon Ice. It's obvious that when it comes to money, betrayal can be seen as a sound business deal to him.*"

"*I'm not following you old man.*"

"*He wanted you to do to Ice what he had already done to you.*"

It was a simple observation but slowly the scales that covered my eyes began to fall off.

"*See Kay, what you fail to realize is that in this treacherous game those guys are dinosaurs. You're what twenty years old now? In their minds you and your whole generation is like the fuckin' Ice Age-ya follow?*"

"*The Ice Age?*"

"*Yeah, that's what killed off the dinosaurs. Don't smile this is real talk here. Everyone who comes in contact with you can feel your energy and see your potential. When the dinosaurs look at you they see the hunger, they see the gift and it scares them. So they put aside their petty differences and ban together in a common cause to first see if they could control you and if not then destroy you. Dice knew you were in the Bahamas so they decided to test your team's loyalty. I'm willing to bet that the plan wasn't to actually take the spot from you; it was a ploy to bring you into conformity. Unfortunately, they didn't count on Ice. It was a bluff that backfired. And since you refuse to back down, it's spinning out of control. Doc, probably needs Ice's head to keep the confidence of his troops and so Dice calls you in attempt to get the head.*"

"*Man that head is attached to my Comrade! Fuck is these jokers thinking?*"

"*They're thinking...they're thinking they have to at all costs, stop you from becoming the center of gravity.*"

"*The what?*"

"*The center of gravity.*"

I began laughing not sure how to respond. Handbone continued.

"*Yeah Kay, I know it may be a little difficult but try to rap your mind around this concept; in every walk of life, politics, war, sports, business etc., there are always people who do what they do just a little better than the others. But in each generation someone comes along with an energy that binds*

everyone around them to them. Like Hannibal, Shaka, like Harriet, like Garvey, Martin, like Malcolm, Marley, Che, Albizo, like Ali and Jordan. When you talk of war the name Hannibal must come to mind. When you talk about basketball Jordan must be mentioned."
"So what you saying...when you talk about hustling my name will be spoken of?"
"Who says hustling is your final destination? What is it that you hustling for?"
"Truthfully?"
"Yeah truthfully."
"Man I'm hustling for power. I want the power to be able to do whatever I want."
"Kay, you have the potential to change the game."
"Man you started drinking again? I come over here to shoot these thoughts at you and you're comparing me to revolutionaries and shit. I'm just a crook."
"I'm comparing you to greatness!"
"What's next?...You gonna tell me Darth Vader is really my old man"
I quipped. Handbone looked offended.
"By that silly statement it's obvious Kay, power is easier to access than wisdom."

I left Handbone's crib still not sure of Dice's motive, yet convinced Dice was the *Phantom of the Opera* and therefore my enemy. But no longer was he a shadow. Unknowingly he was about to be pimped, about to become my double agent-my minister of disinformation. That is-until he and Sam's severance package could be negotiated.

I guess no one ever told Ice the saying *a hard head makes a sore behind* applies to everyone. As if our conversation never took place, he began showing his face around the city determined to prove to the peacocks that the Ice Man never hides. While coming out of Club Arizona in East New York one night, *Ike* and *Miz*, two colorful peacocks out of Brownsville, struck up a convo with Ice. Ice's need to entertain dudes almost cost him his life.

Their purpose was to rock Ice to sleep with frivolous talk giving Doc's goons time to show up. Fortunately Ice caught on and made his exit without letting on that he knew it was a set up. Ice still refused to grasp the jewel-the hood never roots for the underdog. He continued to make bone head moves. Like the shoot out with some young kats in front of Empire Skating Rink or the fiasco at the Apollo where he gun butted a peacock unconscious. He became a ticking time bomb; a rogue soldier out for glory and fame.

As for me, I was conducting the business of war the way it was supposed to be done. I kept a low profile-an invisible target is an impossible one to hit. With the exception of Ice, my ranks were tight and ready. Leaving Ice to pursue his own delusions of grandeur served its purpose. In fact, I couldn't have crafted a better strategy than the one unfolding. Ice's reckless behavior made him the bait. Word on the street was that Doc had become so obsessed with Ice he placed a $50 G marker on his head. Fifty grand is a lot of money and Ice had so many close calls in one week that I finally had to sit him down and order him to lay low.

The final piece of information fell into place. It cost me $10 G's but it was worth every penny. A stripper by the name of *Chamomile* was the lucky recipient. She and a girlfriend did a private party at one of Papa Doc's houses. I sent Handbone to confirm the location. I then sent a team to begin the surveillance. My first strike would be lethal. Things seemed too good to be true and so I hesitated. I couldn't believe that Doc was this vulnerable. Perhaps if I moved a little sooner, any other face besides-hers would haunt me.

Ice's sister, *Tracy,* lived in the Park Slope section of Brooklyn on a nice residential block in a nice quiet neighborhood. I guess that's why Ice assumed it was a safe haven. Somehow Doc found out the location and sent the wolves. They caught Ice coming out of the house. In his arms was his three year old niece with Tracy and her husband right behind him. Two assassins emerged from under parked cars. Before Ice could register what was taking place the hit was going down. Ice quickly put his niece down and attempted to run, trying to move the battle away from his family. The appearance of a third shooter cut off his escape. Shells erupted from their containers; each bullet carrying the promise of fifty grand. Like so many shootouts in the hood everyone else picks up instead of the intended target.

When the smoke cleared Ice with a bullet in his belly, crouched behind a parked car, gun in his palm not wanting to believe the scene that stood before him. The three killers were escaping on foot but it was Tracy's screams that hypnotized him. Louder than the roars of the canons that recently disturbed the neighborhood's tranquility, Tracy's screams disturbed the soul.

Her husband's head plastered to the front door of the house was nothing compared to the lifeless form of her daughter cradled protectively in her arms.

"Oh God!!! Somebody please help my Baby!!! Not my Baby!!!"

It was then that she caught sight of her brother and began screaming...

"What did you do to me!!??! What did you do to me!!??!"

He was speechless. The unthinkable just occurred. His stomach was on fire. The wails of many sirens grew louder- echoing doom. He knew, if he was gonna avenge this he had to leave immediately. It was a tough decision to make to leave his sister behind in such unbearable pain.

He glanced back at his sister one last time wishing he had the courage to end her suffering right then and there. He didn't. He only had enough left to look down at his munchkin; the most precious person in his life-his niece. Like the newspaper would print in the days that followed he must have found the sad irony in her name: Innocent Heart Matthews. *My God her name was Innocent!* Perhaps he finally found respect in the tragic truth of war: the enemy never wastes time separating the guilty from the Innocent.

Ice made it to my crib bleeding profusely. Luckily Alicia was home and was able to staunch the bleeding. She beeped me and I got there twenty minutes later. The belly shot was life threatening.

"*Kameek, if you don't get him to a hospital fast he's going to bleed to death.*"

Alicia's warning dictated the only route available; in order to save Ice's life I had to get him to a hospital. I carried him to his car and put him in the passenger's seat. Jumping into the driver's seat, with my black leather gloves on I began driving.

"*Hold on Bully. Keep talking. It's going to be all right.*"

"*Nah Kay it's not. It'll never be. I destroyed my own heart-Kay.*"

His voice began cracking.

"*My own heart.*"

Ice was referring to his niece's death; the utter hopelessness in his voice sent a shiver of anguish down my spine. I responded the only way I knew how.

"*Don't worry Bully. We're gonna take fuckin' heads for this.*"

Grimacing, Ice closed his eyes.

"*Kay, you were right. I should have listened to you.*"

I cut him off.

"*Not now Bully. This ain't no time for what if's.*"

Ice began coughing violently, as if the coughing alone was enough to kill him, but he came through. In his own words his life was over. He needed me to promise I would avenge Innocent's death no matter what. My plan was to drive him to Staten Island and leave him and the car in front of the hospital. Ice was falling in and out of consciousness babbling like a baby, a fevered sweat pouring profusely down his face. He was begging Tracy and Innocent for forgiveness when he went under. As I neared the Verrazano Bridge I thought about Ice saving my neck on Rikers and realized I owed him more than abandonment.

I cut down a side street and turned off the engine. He was in tremendous pain but was able to open his eyes long enough to see my muzzle take aim. Perhaps it was just my imagination; a need to numb my conscience. But to this very day I swear, just before I pulled the trigger, Ice mouthed the words... "*Thank you...*"

CHAPTER 18
HIT A KILLER - BE A KILLER

Two days later I was sitting in Papa Doc's mansion. He was prostrated before me in the master bedroom on his white cashmere carpet. Mouth taped shut, hands Boy Scout bound, bewildered. A broken man checkmated in his own fortress by a young buck. His body guard dead two feet away to his left, wife and daughter blind folded and gagged two feet to his right. How symbolic I thought. Handbone led the strike team with deadly precision.

The house was beautiful. A palace full of opulent trappings the likes of which my young eyes saw only on the *Lifestyles of the Rich and Famous.* Imported rugs, water fountains, one-of-a-kind paintings, a truck load worth of expensive artifacts... You name it he probably had it.

The effortless way in which I was able to find myself standing over him became easy to explain. You see, the Prince who spends more on luxury than arms has already lost the throne. Even as I measured my adversary, my team was plundering the palace. Everything of value was being liberated. Like a virgin touched for the very first time his safe opened up revealing its secret treasures. I stood over him grabbed him by the collar and whispered...

"How does it feel?"

His eyes once again began watering up. He looked away. I yanked him back to me.

"Look at me muthafucka when I'm talking to you! Look at me dead in my eyes like a man!"

Finally I saw the anger, the defiance, the warrior flash in his eyes. I was happy to see it and smiled. Still in a whisper...

"Yeah that's right. Die with dignity."

We were eye to eye the way it was supposed to be.

"Just imagine what's gonna happen to those two bitches over there in a few minutes."

That broke him. His sobbing was muffled by the tape around his mouth. As the tears began to flow in torrents down his face, I wrapped the wire around his neck and slowly squeezed the life out of him; all the while looking him dead in his eyes. It was personal. I whispered...

"*Her name was Innocent.*"

A glimmer of recognition registered in his eyes before his pupils found those far away shadows and he was nothing more than a twitching corpse. I walked over to his wife and whispered in her ear.

"*Bury him. Leave town. Never come back. Do you understand me?*"

She did. The smell of her feces and urine running freely on the carpet confirmed her comprehension. Her and her daughter's lives were spared in the same name that her husband's was lost...for Innocent.

By all accounts the funeral was a spectacular event. Covered by all major news agencies, Innocent's death became the rallying cry for a community tired of the crack scourge. Ghettos throughout America were calling for an end to the tyrannical reign of King Crack. The seeds of revolution borne by Innocent's death was underway. Community activists from as far away as Ohio brought bus loads full of parents and their children, to pay respect to the slain child.

A tiny pink coffin, encased in a golden domed carriage, pulled by twenty spotless white ponies slowly made its way down Fulton Street. Both sides of the Bed-Stuy Avenue sidewalks were jammed with people of all shapes, sizes and hues. Businesses were closed and traffic, came to a halt. News cameras caught every angle of the event and beamed these images as far away as California.

I sat in my crib watching the funeral on TV. Unrestricted tears ran down my face for Innocent and my own innocence lost. I was crying for the little boy I used to be. The adventurer who loved bike riding and skelly whose only ambition was to turn the game over in Ms. Pac-Man. For the little boy who learned how to swim at age seven. For the little boy who no matter how hard he tried could not stay up past 11 p.m. For the boy who would curl up in the bed next to his mother seeking protection from the monsters that lurk in the dark and wondering at what point I had become the monster. At what point did I taste the forbidden fruit that took my innocence away?

As the cameras captured images of other people crying, I knew that their cries were not just for the tragedy that stood before them, but also for the tragedy that lived within them. I knew with certainty that my life would not be wasted in the streets. There was something bigger in store for me. My life, just like Innocent's death had meaning. The release of twenty doves signaled the eulogy's ending. I cut off the TV and wiped the tears away. Enough of this mushy shit.

The weeks following the deaths of Innocent, Tracy's husband, Ice and Doc were hectic. 1-I could not afford to leave any stones unturned so I didn't. Meticulously I covered all bases. 2-With Ice's death, homicide was able to close a few cases. They were always good for playing *Pin the Tail on the Donkey*. Ice became the latest in a long line of jackasses used to fill a quota. Now if they could only figure out who killed him.

Strangely, the legend, fame and general stripes Ice sought in life he won in death. Similar to a slain rapper, Ice's life took on mythical proportions. Even the media played their part. An exclusive article outlining Ice's criminal accomplishments including the jewelry heist of Raquel Welch, secured the second page of The Daily News. While on the third page his rap sheet and Rikers Island photo were placed menacingly above quotes from his so called friends, who spoke about his killer instincts and reign of terror. There were even talks of a movie.

Doc's death occurred in Jersey and thus there existed no official link to Ice. But the streets knew better and Doc's death became Ice's final heroic act. According to the hood he avenged his niece's murder despite being shot nine times. If it weren't all so sad and tragic it would've been hilarious. *So this is the stuff legends are made of.*

During the long and restless hours of waiting, when Ice was the bait and the war appeared to be inevitably going to go Doc's way, I was already thinking long and hard about my future after the war. This is not to sound too cocky but I knew that the victory would eventually be mine. Doc was no longer the lion of old. He had grown toothless with a roar more deadly than his bite. By allowing Champ and Dice to con him into a situation without thoroughly examining the battlefield told me all I needed to know; I wasn't up against a Premiere General but a businessman who believed himself insulated by his money. Like Jordan, I knew the fourth quarter belonged to me.

What direction should I take? Should I, by virtue of my victory, take over Doc's position and assume his God Father status? Did I want it? One of the sticking points for me was I wanted no more parts of the drug game. The ability to acquire large quantities of money made it a hard hustle to abandon...but, and there's always a *but*...at what cost does one betray their own conscience?

Everything is not for everyone and though I proved successful; selling drugs I discovered was not for me. Was it my stay at Gail's crib where I came face to face with the devastation my product was causing? Or was it Innocent's murder; a three year old caught not in the cross fire of bullets but-greed. Both experiences pushed me closer to the ledge; yet the final push could've been the prolonged stiffness in my mother's hugs. The disappointment and sadness enshrined in her eyes whenever she directed her gaze my way. Or perhaps it was the day she discovered my chosen occupation and called me an enemy of God. Wow! That's pretty close to being called a devil...right or wrong? Now, I ain't no religious dude but when your moms compares you to Satan it's not a statement easy to shake off. J.B.'s response to my letter referred to me as a savage in the pursuit of happiness. Was I? He also attached this parable from the O.G. Bible:

1) JOSTLE THE PICK POCKET ONCE ASKED THE SON OF MAN
2) "OH VOICE OF GOD, I BESEECH YOU THIS QUESTION FOR I SEEK DIVINE WISDOM   IN THIS PERPLEXING MATTER."

3) THE SON OF MAN TEMPORARILY CEASED PLUCKING DATES FROM A NEIGHBOR'S DATE TREE TO BECOME AN EAR.

4) "SOME PEOPLE CALL ME A THIEF", JOSTLE THE PICK POCKET BEGAN, "TO THIS DESCRIPTION I AM IN CONFLICT. WHILE I DO TAKE WHAT DOES NOT BELONG TO ME, I TAKE ONLY FROM THE ROMANS OUR OPPRESSORS AN AVOWED ENEMY. FOR ALL THAT THEY WROUGHT FROM US; AM I WRONG DEAR VOICE OF GOD AND IF SO HOW?"

5) THE SON OF MAN CONTEMPLATED THIS MATTER FOR A LONG TIME AS HE RESUMED SELECTING THE JUICIEST DATES FOR PICKING. FINALLY HE RESPONDED.

6) "DOES THE HONEY BEE WHO STEALS THE NECTAR FROM THE FLOWER WORRY HIMSELF SO?"

7) "OF COURSE NOT", CAME JOSTLE'S RESPONSE.

8) "SO THEN WHY DO YOU CONCERN YOURSELF WITH THESE MATTERS, UNLESS YOU DO NOT MOVE LIKE THE BEE?"

9) "PLEASE EXPLAIN", REPLIED THE THIEF.

10) "THE BEE STEALS THE NECTAR FROM THE FLOWER, SECRETES IT INTO HONEY AND CONTRIBUTES IT TO THE BUILDING AND MAINTENANCE OF A COMMUNAL HIVE. YES HE STEALS BECAUSE THE NECTAR BELONGS TO THE FLOWER AND NOT THE BEE BUT IT IS A SELFLESS ACT; ONE BORN OUT OF A COMMUNAL NEED.

11) BUT SHOULD THE BEE TAKE THE NECTAR FOR ITS OWN SELFISH PLEASURE, THEN IT IS VANITY THAT CAUSES IT TO ACT AND THE BEE MUST BE TREATED AS A THIEF.

12) AND HOW CAN IT BE OTHERWISE? FOR EVEN WHEN THE FLOWERS ARE NO LONGER IN BLOOM, VANITY WILL STILL BE IN THE HEART BECAUSE IT IS A DISEASE THAT DEFIES ALL SEASONS. THUS IT WILL BE ONLY A MATTER

OF TIME BEFORE THE BEE BEGINS STEALING FROM THE HIVE LEAVING CHAOS AND CONFUSION IN ITS WAKE.

13) TELL ME PICK POCKET HAVE YOU NOT NOTICED THAT I HAVE BEEN GATHERING THESE DATES FOR THE LAST FIVE DAYS?"

14) THE THIEF STILL ABSORBING THE MEANING OF THE SON OF MAN'S WORDS, MERELY SHOOK HIS HEAD AFFIRMATIVELY.

15) THE SON OF MAN CONTINUED. "THE DATE TREE BELONGS TO ANOTHER YET I TAKE THESE DATES WITHOUT PERMISSION. THE OWNER KNOWS BUT HAS NO OBJECTIONS BECAUSE IT IS FROM THESE DATES THAT HE DRINKS THE WINE WHICH PUTS HIM TO BED AT NIGHT PEACEFULLY. FROM THESE DATES THAT I PLUCK THEN GRIND A VARIETY OF MEDICINAL USES FROM PREVENTING EYE DISEASE TO POTENT LAXATIVES ARE BORN. I PLUCK WITHOUT PERMISSION, NOT FOR MYSELF. I TAKE THAT WHICH IS NOT MINE–FOR THE BENEFIT OF US ALL."

16) AND JOSTLE THE PICK POCKET WALKED AWAY IN SHAME BECAUSE THE SON OF MAN HAD ALSO ANSWERED THE GREATER QUESTION. FOR NOW JOSTLE THE PICK POCKET KNEW WITH CERTAINTY THAT HE AND HIS KIND WERE THE CAUSE OF THE CHAOS AND CONFUSION IN THE LAND. HIS HEART WAS TROUBLED BECAUSE THROUGH HIS ACTIONS VANITY BECAME HIS GOD.

*   *   *

I sensed that I was at a crossroads in my life. Success always depends on being decisive and I chose to forsake the triple beam. While not having any intentions on completely getting out of the life, I decided to abandon what to me was the most detestable aspect of it. For the past two years I successfully built a disciplined and focused team. Not one of those superficial jump offs that became popular after the movie *New Jack City* hit the scene. What began as just a thought quickly bore flesh; an idea transformed into a machine-my machine.

I decided to take my team into the pressure game. Extortion is an ancient profession based on the art of persuasion. It's about being able to convince your mark that it is in their best interest to cooperate with your law and order. Our motto: *Squeeze until they squirm, double up on the grip and squeeze some more.* We would target peacocks. Their love for luxury would make them easy and predictable prey. Their only option would be either to conform or lose their lives. Resistance would not be tolerated but obliterated.

That was the mandate I gave my team when I sat them down and explained the direction I was heading. With the exception of *Bizzy*, they all decided to cast their lots with me. Bizzy wanted to stay his hand in the drug game. He was a loyal soldier who served his general well and as a reward I gave him the L.E.S. spot to do with as he pleased; but even he wouldn't be exempt from his monthly tribute.

Explaining to the team if we moved correctly, covering all our bases and remained under the radar, killing peacocks would be a task easily avoided. Our success would depend on our ability to secure accurate information. With accurate information we would always have the advantage. It was time to hump the game for longevity and leave the quick nut to the nuts. Looking around at the other contenders I saw no team on the board that could remotely withstand my onslaught. They were all peacocks.

The 64 squares that made up the game board looked the same to us all. Yet they were stuck playing Checkers while I was determined to play Chess. Even when the king is defeated, there are those who find honor in continued resistance. Their ambitions had to be surgically clipped if I was to truly capitalize off the victory and become-the center of gravity. Ask any weatherman and they will tell you it is difficult to predict and prepare for a storm you have no idea is coming. I was that storm and the peacocks had no fuckin' idea.

*   *   *

Meanwhile in the Riverdale section of the Bronx the O.G. Saquan stepped out of his two story house to find an Armani suitcase on his porch. Immediately growing suspicious he ordered his right hand man to put his ear to it and see if the shit was ticking. After establishing that it probably wasn't a bomb he carried the suitcase into the house and closed the door. Upon examining the suitcase they noticed the name Mr. and Mrs. François was stitched into the leather handle. Initially Saquan couldn't place the name, but then it hit him and it hit him hard. That was the birth name of his late Comrade Papa Doc. Saquan received the sad news the morning before and already began making the necessary inquiries into locating the culprits behind Doc's murder. Saquan was to the Bronx what Doc was to Brooklyn and Queens. They came up the ranks together, clawing their way to respectability.

"We put our work in, we paid our dues..."

He and Doc would always remind each other. Revenging Doc's death was something he had to do because he knew if the roles had been reversed Doc would've undoubtedly done the same. So far his inquiries were met with a hood wall of silence. Perhaps Doc knew he was about to die and sent the suitcase. All these thoughts ran through his mind before finally telling his right hand man to...

"Open the damned thing. Let's see what we got."

As soon as the suitcase opened an overwhelming stench of sour meat assaulted their senses. Both men began vomiting uncontrollably. Saquan had been in the game for over thirty years and never before had he felt the sheer terror coursing through his veins as he was feeling at that very moment. Still not believing what he was seeing he vomited once more. Three human heads, faces contorted in eternal pain sat on blood soaked newspapers. None of this made any sense. Saquan had no clue who these men were but felt sorry for them. Not because they were dead, but because clearly their deaths had been painful.

Saquan noticed a golden envelope tucked into the corner of the case. Quickly he opened and read it desperate to know what the hell was going on. When he was done he just stared at the words–finally agreeing with his wife.

"I'm getting too old for this shit."

It was at that moment that Saquan finally decided to retire. Saquan's hand began to shake uncontrollably. His right hand man observing Saquan's cowardice snatched the note card away from Saquan and read its contents...

      THREE LITTLE PIGGIES BUILT THEIR FOUNDATION FROM STRAW-SIDING WITH DOC. THE FIRE THEY NEVER SAW, UNTIL IT CONSUMED THEM UP. THEIR HEADS ARE YOUR TROPHIES TO DO WITH WHAT YOU LIKE. THREE LITTLE PIGGIES, CHAMP, SAM AND DICE.

      P.S. HERE'S A RIDDLE FOR AN O.G. TO CONSIDER. QUIT WHILE YOU'VE A HEAD. GET IT? FIRST AND FINAL WARNING.

      THE CENTER OF GRAVITY

*   *   *

NEWARK, NEW JERSEY

In a previous incarnation she responded to the name Precious but now to her associates and underlings she was known as Peaches. While in the gritty and often sinister streets of Newark she was euphemistically referred to, by the name that appeared on every bag of heroin in Weeqaic and Hooterville-the **Queen**.
   A figure of controversy and drama since her arrival 4 ½ years prior; considered a phantom, rarely seen yet undeniably felt. Having ushered in a reign of terror on an already ravaged land, her meteoric rise to the top of Brick City's underworld was nothing short of relentless. Relentless and ruthless. So much so, many suspected a federal or local indictment to fall any day.
   The Mayor of Newark declared, on local news, an all out war against the so called **Queen and her minions**. *To his credit, like most politicians promising no new taxes, he really believed, momentarily at least, his own rhetoric. But the devil is always in the details and there were a few devilish details that promised to derail his declaration of war. For starters the Queen was elusive. As thorough as Peaches was in her ruthlessness she proved equally efficient in her stealth. The invisible virus is what the local law enforcement called her. Yet as careful as she was, as cautious as she had been; she knew, the way any uninvited houseguest does - she overstayed her welcome. It was just a matter of time before the rug would be violently yanked from underneath her. Time to return home.*
   Peaches, the undisputed Queen of Newark, sat pensively in the study room of her home in the Montclair section of New Jersey. Above all others she loved this room the most. Its tranquility seemed organic - a place for the weary mind and heart. Carefully weighing all her options she surrendered to the peace. Minutes melted serenely into hours, as Peaches sat comfortably in her camel skin recliner oblivious to the rest of her surroundings. Alone with her thoughts...and her fears. The

pitter-patter of tiny footsteps followed closely by the thumping of heavier ones broke her concentration.

Her five year old son Kameer bolted into the room laughing hysterically. Running hard - his thirteen year old Aunt Jazmeen trailing in hot pursuit. Peaches smiled, (look at my son, already running from the law) her outstretched arms told Kameer that he was almost there, almost safe, almost - but not quite.

Just as his tiny fingers reached out to grab hold of hers he suddenly found himself airborne. Jazmeen's powerful arms lifted him up and effortlessly back into her bosom.

"Not so fast big head", his aunt whispered in his ear. Kameer continued to laugh all the while resisting his captor's embrace.

"You know your son is something else don't you. I mean you can't take you eyes off him for a second."

Jazmeen pretended to be exasperated - but since this chase and catch scenario, this battle of wills, had become a nightly routine; Peaches knew her little sister enjoyed it just as much at Kameer. A stab of anxiety entered her belly. Is the time right? Asking herself this question for the tenth time.

Just as Peaches wrestled Kameer from her sister's arms her younger brother Andre, as if on cue, entered the room. Peaches' heart soared. All that I hold dear is in this room - my family - I did it all for ya. Andre just turned sixteen and was due to graduate from high school in four months. He received academic scholarship offers from a dozen different colleges but was seriously considering two; Lincoln and Temple Universities.

Her sister was also excelling in school. Jazmeen was the captain of her debate team and quickly becoming a rising volleyball star who loved school with a passion. Both her siblings were good kids - oblivious to all the pain Peaches caused in their name. How would their lives turned out if I hadn't taken the initiative to make a better one for them?

No. She harbored no regrets - only demons and enemies. And it was time to confront them both. She hadn't expected him to win the war but he had. Even after she provided Doc with Ice's whereabouts, Kameek proved too much for him.

Papa Doc had been utterly defeated and the streets of N.Y.C. had a new champion - a new star. Shit, he would make way for the Queen or else - or else what? This is where her plans always drew a blank. Are you cold enough to kill him? Looking deep into her son's beautiful brown eyes she knew it was time to face her number one enemy - Am I ready to face your Father", she whispered.

*   *   *

EPILOGUE

"Kameek Barnes, Kameek Barnes..."
"Hey Officer Smithy...what's up?"
"Who were you just talking to?"
"Myself...you know how this solitary begins to play tricks on the mind."
"Yeah. Well listen...the Judge wants you back in the courtroom pronto."
"They reached a verdict?"
"No. The Jury has requested another read back."
"Really? Who is it this time?"
"Your brother's."
Son of a bitch!
"Ayat Smithy. Give me a second to freshen up."
"Look Kameek. I'm not trying to be an asshole but you know how Judge Kramer can get. Pronto means pronto with him."
"Yeah well pronto is going to have to mean a minute Smithy. It's just that simple."
"All right Kameek. I'll be back in a minute."
"Thank you. I'll be ready."

So it all boils down to Jamal's testimony...Do they dare place the keys to my freedom-in my brother's hands? The irony of fate-the irony of fate...

* * *

Oh pardon me my friend, as you can see I gotta run back to this courtroom for a second-it shouldn't take long. I tell you what, consider all that I have shared with you this far but please-please, reserve your judgment. This story is nowhere near complete.

*   *   *

"Kameek Barnes..."
"Yeah Smithy..."
"Judge Kramer is waiting."
Fuck Judge Kramer!
"Ayat Smithy. Let's go. I'm ready."
Hey you...don't forget...I'll be right back.

*   *   *